Danger in Dead Man's Mine

Danger in Dead Man's Mine

DAVE GLAZE

COTEAU
BOOKS
FOR KIDS

This novel is a work of fiction. Names, characters, places, and incidents either are the product of the author's imagination or are used fictitiously. Any resemblance to actual persons, living or dead, is coincidental.

Edited by Laura Peetoom
Cover images by Corbis.ca and iStockphoto.com
Cover montage and design by Erin Woodward
Book design by Duncan Campbell
Printed and bound in Canada by Transcontinental Printing

Library and Archives Canada Cataloguing in Publication

Glaze, Dave, 1947-
    Danger in Dead Man's Mine / Dave Glaze.

(1912: The Mackenzie Davis files; 3)
ISBN 978-1-55050-416-3

    I. Title. II. Series: Glaze, Dave, 1947- . 1912: The Mackenzie
Davis files.

PS8563.L386D35 2009   jC813'.54   C2009-903411-5

10   9   8   7   6   5   4   3   2   1

2517 Victoria Avenue
Regina, Saskatchewan
Canada S4P 0T2

Available in Canada from:
Publishers Group Canada
9050 Shaughnessy Street
Vancouver, BC, V6P 6E5

The publisher gratefully acknowledges the financial support of its publishing program by: the Saskatchewan Arts Board, the Canada Council for the Arts, the Government of Canada through the Book Publishing Industry Development Program (BPIDP), and the City of Regina Arts Commission.

For Ellis

CHAPTER ONE
Monday, August 19, 1912

Keeping his head down, Mackenzie followed Francis deeper into the deserted mine. With each step they took away from the sun-filled entrance, the coal black walls seemed to suck up more light. The air turned chilly and damp and smelled musty, like a dirt-walled basement.

Mackenzie stumbled over a rock hidden in the shadows. Reaching out to catch his balance, he skinned his knuckles on one of the roughly sawn posts that lined the sides of the shaft. "Ow," he murmured.

"You all right?" Francis asked. "Do you want to stop?"

"No," Mackenzie said. Not as long as I can see a little bit, he told himself. And – he glanced over his shoulder – I can find the way out.

"Aren't you worried about cracking your noggin?"

Mackenzie asked. He could feel his cap grazing against the heavy braces held up by the posts. And Francis was at least two heads taller than him.

"So far, so good," Francis said.

"Is that water I hear?" Mackenzie didn't like the way his voice had changed inside the tunnel. It seemed weak, swallowed up by the rock.

"It's trickling down the walls," Francis said. "Father says there's always water underground. Sometimes there's so much, it's like a little river running down the shaft to the entrance."

"No one uses this for mining anymore, right?" Mackenzie asked. "The coal's all gone?"

"The men who built this mine would have taken out everything they could get at," Francis said. "First they dug out what they called rooms, except they left big pillars of coal to hold up the ceilings. Then they knocked down the pillars and hoped they could get the coal out before the ceilings came crashing down on them. After they left, other men would have picked over everything they could scavenge. Then it was abandoned."

Mackenzie raised his hands to touch the roof. "What about *this* ceiling?" he asked.

"A mine entry like this was always braced really well when it was built," Francis said. "But over years, lots of the old timbers will have fallen down. Parts of it probably have collapsed further back in the mine." They stopped walking.

"We shouldn't go any further without a safety lamp," Francis said.

"What's that?"

"It gives you some light," Francis said, "and the way it burns can tell a miner when there are dangerous gases in the air. You don't want to be near the damp. It can explode and kill you."

Mackenzie didn't want to think about explosions and ceilings crashing down. He decided he'd never come in here with anyone except Francis. Not even with Albert or any of his other friends at home.

"Have we gone far enough?" Francis asked.

"Yes," Mackenzie said.

WALKING OUT OF THE MINE, the boys squinted into the blinding sunlight that lit the bottom of a steep-sided canyon on the edge of Lethbridge. Footpaths and wagon trails meandered between the groves of trees and bushes that grew on the flat plain of the Belly River. Francis chose one.

"The city goes right to the tip of the valley here," he said, skirting around burnt tin cans, broken boards, and the scattered shards of a glass bottle that had been smashed against a rock. "It's easy for people to come down and get a look inside this mine."

"Like me," Mackenzie said. "You remembered."

"Of course," Francis said. "When you visited us at Bellevue all we could find on the mountain were caves we *pretended* were mines. Finally I get to show you a real one."

"And so soon!" Mackenzie laughed. "We just got here. Our mothers probably don't even know we're gone."

"They're sisters," Francis said. "And they have the baby to talk about. They're not thinking about us."

"Are there more old mines down here?" Mackenzie asked.

"Yes, but I don't know where." Francis stopped and pointed up. "Look," he said.

A thick, black beam soared across the canyon above the treetops. It was a railway bridge, but Mackenzie couldn't see anything holding it up. It seemed like it was floating on air.

"What's that?" he asked.

"The High Level Bridge," Francis said. "Lethbridge is famous for it. Longest trestle bridge in the world. A mile from one side of the valley to the other."

"Our train didn't go across it," Mackenzie said.

"No," Francis said. "The bridge is on the west side of town. You came in from the east. You'd have known if you'd gone over it. The engineer slows down and people in the coaches start oohhing and awing."

"I give up," Mackenzie said, "where are the trestles?"

"On the other side of those cottonwoods," Francis said. "I'll show you."

The trail led into a meadow where a double line of

giant steel piers marched like a parade of soldiers across the valley.

"From further away," Francis said, "the piers are hidden by the trees. It isn't until you're really close that you see them."

It would be hard to miss them from here, Mackenzie thought. Craning his neck, he followed the criss-crossing steel plates of the bridge pylons as they rose higher and higher to support the wooden base that held the railway tracks. "Holy smoke!"

"Three hundred feet high," Francis said. "From up there you can see clear to the mountains and everything that's going on in the valley."

Striding across the field, Mackenzie and Francis startled thousands of clattering grasshoppers into the air. On the far side, the boys joined a trail so well-travelled the plants had been beaten flat and the ground pounded into dust. Gritty brown clouds rose with each step.

Mackenzie brushed away the insects that had stuck like burrs to his clothing. Reaching behind Mackenzie's back, Francis flicked a hopper from his cousin's shoulder.

"When did you grow so much?" Mackenzie asked. "Your arms must be twice as long as mine. How tall are you?"

"Over six feet," Francis said, grinning. "Mother says I had a growth spurt."

"You're only fifteen years old!" Mackenzie said.

"And already big enough to be a miner. Is that what you want?" he asked. "Is that what you're going to do?"

Francis shook his head. "No," he said.

"Then, what?"

"I'm not telling yet."

Francis's voice sounded different, Mackenzie thought, more serious. He was almost four years older than Mackenzie, but the two of them had always shared secrets. Why were things different, all of a sudden? he wondered.

THE PATH VEERED TOWARD the side of the valley and they heard the sound of squeaking wheels and jangling steel chains. Prancing saddle horses, huffing motorcars, and other hardy people on foot led the boys up the road out of the valley. In front of them, a wagon heavily loaded with grain made slow progress, the horses straining to advance up the hill. A railway tie was chained to the wagon and pulled in the dirt behind the back wheels. The teamster called to his horses to ease off. The wagon stopped and then rolled a couple of feet backwards until the wheels jammed against the tie. Feeling the weight released from their shoulders, the horses relaxed in their harnesses.

Near the top, the road climbed through a coulee and passed a dusty brickyard. When they reached the flat prairie, the boys could see clouds billowing from a trio of tall brick smokestacks that towered above a cluster of wooden buildings.

"That's Galt Number Three Mine," Francis said. "She's running full steam again, at last. Everything was shut down by the strike for over a year. Do you see that tall building? It's the head frame. That's where the hoist is that brings men and coal up from underground."

The road ahead split. In one direction, it ran across a meadow before meeting Ninth Street and climbing onto a bridge built over the busy railway tracks near the train station. The other way led to long rows of identical small white bungalows.

"And that," Francis said, "is also called Number Three."

The company houses were sparse, with plenty of space between the buildings, as if many houses had been planted on the dry grassland but only these few had come up.

"During the worst of the strike," Francis went on, "we hardly had bread for the table. There was just no money."

"What did you do?" Mackenzie asked.

"My father got odd jobs when he could. I left school for awhile. It's hard, Mackenzie, when no one's bringing home a pay packet. I don't want my family to go through that again."

Behind one house, an old man, his back bent and his shoulders stooped low, slowly swept the planks that made a sidewalk to his outhouse. Swinging his head toward the road, the man studied the boys before giving them a stiff wave.

Pointing to a house with blue trim around the windows and doors, Francis left the road and took a shortcut across a vacant lot.

"Uncle Jimmy must be happy to be back at work," Mackenzie said.

Francis shot him a glance. "He would have been," he said. "Father hasn't set foot in the mine since the day the strike started."

EVERYTHING STOPPED, Mackenzie learned at supper, when Uncle Jimmy started coughing. It's like, he thought, it wouldn't be polite to talk or laugh or eat when his uncle could barely breathe. The coughing came from deep in his chest. Each hacking spasm sounded like it was tearing away part of his lungs. Holding a stained handkerchief to his mouth to catch what he spit up, Uncle Jimmy winced with each cough and each rattling intake of breath.

At the other end of the table, Mackenzie's mother seemed to be studying the bowl of pudding she was about to serve. His baby sister Nellie had spotted the dessert from her mother's lap and fidgeted to be fed. Their foreheads wrinkled with identical frowns, mother and daughter did not want to wait much longer.

Mackenzie's mother put a few spoonfuls of pudding

into her own bowl and gave Nellie a taste. One of his mother's ears, Mackenzie knew, would be cocked toward the nearby bedroom where his Aunt Betsy waited for her baby to be born. Mackenzie's mother was here to assist with that delivery; Mackenzie had come to help with Nellie. His father's job with *The Daily Phoenix* had kept him in Saskatoon.

Francis rested his eyes on his plate and his hands on the table. Seated beside him, Mackenzie copied his stance. Across from them sat Mackenzie's cousin Ruth. She was twelve years old, like Mackenzie, and waiting for her own growth spurt. Ruth, Mackenzie saw, was the only one in the room ready to hand her father a glass of water. Next to her was cousin John Walter's empty chair. Eight years of age, Mackenzie thought, was hardly old enough to be skipping meals.

With a final sputtering cough, Uncle Jimmy grew quiet. Mackenzie stole a peek at his uncle. Francis looked just like his father, Mackenzie thought. Curly blond hair hung over their foreheads and ears. Crinkly laugh lines spread from the corners of their eyes. Their square chins were dimpled.

Uncle Jimmy wiped his lips, stuffed the cloth into his pocket, and scraped his chair away from the table. Walking across the kitchen, he pushed open the back screen door and let it slap shut behind him.

Mackenzie's mother wiped Nellie's face and handed her to Mackenzie. "There's dessert," she said cheerily. "Ruth made it. Tapioca. It's quite tasty."

Mackenzie had stirred the pudding. His mother was being polite. The top might look edible but the bottom was scorched to the pan.

"No, thank you." Francis stood up. He walked down a short hallway and into the half-open door to his mother's bedroom.

"Ruth?" Picking up a small bowl, Mackenzie's mother dished in two large spoonfuls.

Ruth took the dessert and began to eat.

"Yes, please," Mackenzie said, when his mother turned to him. "Just a bit. I'm not too hungry."

"I'd certainly like some," Mackenzie's mother said. "And I know your mother would, too, Ruth. I'll take it in to her in a minute."

Aunt Betsy hadn't left her room since Mackenzie and his family had arrived that morning. He had heard her talking quietly to his mother or to Ruth, but he hadn't set eyes on her. The baby, he knew, was due any day.

Francis left his mother's bedroom, walked through the kitchen without glancing toward the table, and pushed through the outside door. Mackenzie's mother picked up a bowl of pudding and headed to the bedroom. Pulling the serving bowl closer, Ruth spooned more dessert into her bowl. Mackenzie held a spoon to Nellie's lips.

Ruth was the cousin Mackenzie had spent the least time with. He felt odd asking her a question, but he wanted to know.

"What's going on?" he asked.

"Father's had a bee in his bonnet for hours," Ruth said. "All he could talk about was how happy this was going to make Francis. He could hardly stand the wait until you two came home."

"Francis doesn't look very delighted to me," Mackenzie said.

Ruth stood up and began stacking dirty dishes on her arm. "He knew it was coming," she said. "He could've done something about it."

Mackenzie watched his cousin add plates to the piles already spread across the counter. Curious about what Francis and Uncle Jimmy were talking about outside, he tried to think of some reason to follow them. Handfuls of cutlery crashed into the dishpan. Maybe, Mackenzie thought, I can get Ruth to tell me more. Setting his sister on the floor, he gathered in the cups and took them to the counter.

TWO DAMP TEA TOWELS WERE discarded over the back of a kitchen chair. Mackenzie picked up a serving bowl Ruth had washed, whipped the third towel over the inside, and set the bowl on a cupboard shelf. The last time he had visited this family, Aunt Betsy had directed everything in the kitchen.

"Do you always do this by yourself?" he asked.

"John Walter's supposed to help," Ruth said. "But he's good at sneaking away after meals. Or not even showing up to eat here."

"Where was he today?"

"You haven't met Alfred yet?"

"No," Mackenzie said.

"You will," Ruth said. "Those two are like the Siamese twins you see at the circus. Always stuck together."

"What do they do?"

"Don't know," Ruth said. "John Walter's always done whatever he feels like. It's worse when Mother's sick and can't keep track of him. He won't listen to me."

"And Francis?"

"He's no help," Ruth said. "Maybe if he'd box his brother's ears once in awhile, John Walter would pay attention. But Francis wouldn't. He's too nice."

"Is your mother all right?" Mackenzie asked. It felt odd that he hadn't seen Aunt Betsy yet. She always made a fuss over him. No matter how old he got, she insisted on kissing him when she first saw him

"She doesn't want you to see her big belly," Ruth said. "She wants to have the baby first and then show him off."

"When will that be?"

"Mrs. Giles will only say, 'soon.' She's the midwife."

"Don't you have a doctor?" Mackenzie asked. "When Nellie and I were born, there was always a doctor." It was only a year since Nellie's birth. Mackenzie could remember what the doctor had said. "He told my mother it wasn't safe to use a midwife."

"Mackenzie," Ruth said, shaking her hands and drying them on her worn blue dress, "doctors cost money. We don't have any money. My father hasn't worked for months. You heard him coughing. He's too sick. He can hardly breathe."

"What about when he gets better?"

Ruth stared at Mackenzie. "You ever hear of black lung?" she asked.

You could die from black lung, Mackenzie knew. It was caused by the coal dust that miners breathe in when they're underground. Mackenzie remembered rubbing his fingers on the bottom of their empty coal bin at home. The dust felt smooth. It smudged on his skin. When it settled in the miners' chests, it coated the insides of their lungs. "Yes," he said.

"No one knows if he's going to get any better," Ruth said.

Mackenzie tried to imagine what it would be like if his father didn't work. How would they eat? Would I have to get a job? he wondered. His friend Stanley didn't have a father and he had to quit school to work for Mr. Lavallée on his dray.

Thinking back to what happened after supper, Mackenzie asked, "Does this have anything to do with what Uncle Jimmy is talking to Francis about?"

"You'll have to ask them yourself," Ruth said, pushing the dirty pots into the dishwater. "No one tells me anything."

MACKENZIE GRIPPED THE HANDLE of the screen door but he didn't push it open. There was at least an hour of sunlight left and Uncle Jimmy was still outside. Mackenzie could see him lying flat on his back with his hands clasped behind his head. From twenty feet away, Uncle Jimmy's breathing sounded like an ogre growling deep in his cave.

Mackenzie thought his uncle seemed to have shrunk. He looked shorter and not as fierce as Mackenzie remembered. Whenever Uncle Jimmy returned from a shift at the mine, coal dust had always burrowed into his ears and filled the wrinkles on his face. It clung to the hollows around his eyes, to the webs between his fingers, and to the sheltered spaces underneath his fingernails. Tonight the man looked pale and sickly.

There was no sign of Francis. Whatever he and his father had spoken about, their talk was finished now. What was Uncle Jimmy doing out there? Mackenzie wondered. What was he thinking about? Was he going to be one of the miners who died from black lung?

Walking into the kitchen, Mackenzie saw the copy of the *Lethbridge Daily Herald* his mother had bought at the station that morning. It reminded him of his father back in Saskatoon. Before he left, Mackenzie's father had given him a small box of cigars to take to a friend who worked at the *Herald*. I'll do that tomorrow, Mackenzie thought, before the baby's born. Turning up the wick on a kerosene lamp, he opened the newspaper.

HOURS LATER, MACKENZIE WOKE with his face pressed against the warm plaster of the wall beneath a small upstairs window. He was sharing John Walter's cot. When his younger cousin had shown up, Uncle Jimmy had sent him in to talk to his mother. He was still in there when Mackenzie had gone to bed. But he could feel him now, curled up against his back. Wiping sweat from his cheek, Mackenzie pried his elbow into the mattress and pushed himself high enough to see out the window.

The dull light from a quarter moon silvered the neighbour's houses and stiffened the plants in Aunt Betsy's garden into stone. A train locomotive huffed slowly away from the station, and then quickly picked up speed on its way east across the flat prairie. The train's whistle wailed a sad goodbye.

A rabbit bounded onto the grass behind the house, stopped for a moment to sniff the air, and then zigzagged toward the garden. Pausing again, the rabbit perked its ears and raised its snout. Satisfied there were no threats, the rabbit disappeared beneath the leafy stalks.

From the kitchen where Uncle Jimmy had laid out a mattress came the sound of a single barking cough, and then a snarl that refused to let the cough worsen. A woman moaned – Aunt Betsy, Mackenzie decided – and a moment later Mackenzie's mother's calm voice drifted up the stairway.

Shifting onto his other elbow, Mackenzie peered across the tiny room. Francis was sleeping in his bed.

When did he come home? Mackenzie wondered. Looking closer, he saw Francis was still wearing his clothes. He must have stayed out really late, Mackenzie thought, if he was too tired to get undressed.

A cool breeze rushed in the window, raising goose bumps on Mackenzie's arms. Nudging John Walter toward the other side of the bed, Mackenzie lay back down. He looked forward to tomorrow. He and his older cousin had plans to keep exploring the valley. Smiling, Mackenzie pulled up the sheet and closed his eyes.

Lethbridge Daily Herald

MONDAY, AUGUST 19, 1912

OLD SOL SMILES ON LETHBRIDGE

Happy Sun Heats Prairies to 100 Degrees

Old Sol is grinning on the grand province of Alberta today and his happy times will last at least one more week. All over the south, the temperatures are reaching one hundred degrees daily. The city of Lethbridge is no exception as the sales of ice chests for mothers and ice cream for fathers and children hit all-time highs.

Tired of heating the prairies only, Old Sol has turned his fiery attention on the Rocky Mountain foothills to our west. On the weekend past, the temperature soared over the hills until hot air met cold and lightning lit the heavens. For hours after, heavy black clouds dropped torrents of rain on the parched grasses. The sudden downpour has swollen the creeks and rivulets that are the sources of the Belly River. In a few days time when these muddy waters reach the city, we may see our Belly stretch its shores.

CHAPTER TWO
Tuesday, August 20, 1912

The next morning, Mackenzie crawled over a dead-to-the-world John Walter to get out of bed. Gathering up his clothes, he sat on Francis's empty cot to get dressed. When he went downstairs, he found his mother alone in the kitchen with Nellie. Holding the baby in one arm, she dipped her fingers into the stove reservoir to see if the water was hot enough for dishes.

"Get yourself some porridge," she said to Mackenzie as she walked to the table. Sitting down, she shifted Nellie onto her lap and pulled a cup of tea toward her.

Mackenzie found three bowls on the counter. One for him, he decided, and one for John Walter. Who else hadn't eaten yet? He dished oatmeal from a pot on the stove into one bowl, added four spoons of butter, and joined his mother.

"Francis is gone," she said, studying her cup.

"Mmm," Mackenzie said, his mouth full of porridge. His cousin was almost an adult. It wouldn't be unusual if he were away from the house once in awhile. "I can wait for him," Mackenzie said.

"It's not like that," his mother said. "Francis is *gone*. He left sometime in the night. He took some clothes with him and put a note on the table for his mother. I haven't read the note, but it surprised your uncle and made him very angry. After pacing in the yard for a time, he went to the mine with the morning shift. He hasn't returned, yet."

"Uncle Jimmy went back to work?" Mackenzie asked.

"No," his mother said, "not to work. He had to talk to someone at the mine."

"Where is Francis?" Mackenzie asked. "Where would he go?"

"I don't think he gave his parents any clues," his mother said, "only that he was leaving."

Would he really do that? Mackenzie wondered. Just up and take off and not tell me? Not even say goodbye? "We were going to go back to the valley today," he said.

"I'm sorry, Mackenzie," his mother said. "His parents feel bad for you, too."

"It has something to do with Uncle Jimmy not working, doesn't it?" Mackenzie said in a low voice. When his mother didn't respond, he went on. "They don't have any money, you know. Uncle Jimmy and Aunt Betsy."

Raising her eyebrows, Mackenzie's mother said, "Really, Mackenzie! That's not your affair."

"Uncle Jimmy hasn't worked for over a year," Mackenzie said. "Did you know that?"

"Yes." His mother frowned. "Aunt Betsy never said as much in her letters but I gathered that." Whispering, she added, "I brought a little extra money. Aunt Betsy will use it for groceries while we're here. But don't ever mention it, Mackenzie. Aunt Betsy hasn't told Uncle Jimmy. He would never allow her to keep it."

"Why?"

Waving her hand, Mackenzie's mother refused to answer his question.

"Forget about Uncle Jimmy for a moment," she said. "You have a job to do while we're in Lethbridge. Do you remember what it is?"

Mackenzie nodded. The box of cigars was stashed under John Walter's bed. "Francis was going to take me to the *Herald* office," he said.

"Well, he won't anymore," his mother said.

Mackenzie could picture the *Herald* reporter from the times Mr. Smith had visited his father. A short man with a balding head and an untrimmed moustache that hung well below his chin, he kept a pocket full of candies he liked to share with anyone he met.

"I'll go there today sometime," Mackenzie said.

Aunt Betsy's weak voice called from the bedroom. Handing over Nellie, Mackenzie's mother went to check on her.

"Aunt Betsy is asking about you," she said, returning to the kitchen. "She'd like a little visit."

"I thought I wasn't supposed to go in there," Mackenzie said. "Aunt Betsy doesn't want me to see her pregnant."

Smiling, his mother said, "She must have changed her mind."

The room beyond the door was darkened by a blanket hung over the window. No breeze from outside had cooled it overnight, and the room was stuffy and hot.

"Mackenzie." Aunt Betsy lay on her back, her head and shoulders propped up with pillows, her hair damp and sticking to her glistening forehead. Mackenzie thought her belly looked as puffy as if she had pushed one or two more pillows under the sheet.

"Come close," Aunt Betsy said. "You're the spitting image of your grandfather, Mackenzie. You and John Walter. All of you stand just like that with your head tilted to the side when you're wondering what to do next."

"That's what my mother says," Mackenzie said.

Aunt Betsy lifted her hand and let if fall onto the bed. She wants me to hold it, Mackenzie realized. He took her warm, moist fingers in his and she tugged him nearer.

"I'm not going to try and kiss you, " Aunt Betsy said. "I have enough sense left to not do that. I just want to know how you're making out here. You've never been in Lethbridge before."

"I'm fine," Mackenzie said.

"No, you're not," Aunt Betsy said, smiling. "You're disappointed Francis isn't here. You were expecting to go to the river valley with him. I can't bring Francis back but I am going to have John Walter show you around instead. I told him it wouldn't hurt if he spent a little less time with Alfred while you're visiting."

I don't want my eight-year-old cousin telling me what to do, Mackenzie thought. I want to be with Francis.

"John Walter won't mind," Aunt Betsy said. "And –" she lowered her voice "– if you're with him you can see what he's getting up to. He's used to coming and going as he pleases, Mackenzie. Ever since he was a toddler. He likes to think he's much older than he really is." She squeezed Mackenzie's hand. "Will you?"

Mackenzie knew as long as Francis was away, he didn't have a choice who he went with. "Sure," he said.

"Oh!" Aunt Betsy cried suddenly. "There! Do you want to feel him? He's kicking like a mule. Right here." She guided Mackenzie's hand over the sheet. "Feel it?"

"Yes," Mackenzie said. It made him feel queasy. He pulled his hand away.

"Thank you, Mackenzie," Aunt Betsy said. "I know you'll keep a good watch on him." Closing her eyes, she said, "I need a nap. I get so tired I could fall asleep while I'm talking."

MACKENZIE HEARD THE SOUND OF footsteps coming down the stairs and his youngest cousin ambled into the room. "There's porridge," Mackenzie said, pointing to the stove. He clinked two spoons together and then handed them to his sister to play with.

Wearing faded black pants and a red-and-black checked shirt, John Walter scraped the bottom of the pot and ate the last of the oatmeal from the serving spoon. From the way John Walter kept his eyes on the hallway to his mother's room, Mackenzie was sure his cousin wasn't usually allowed to do that.

"Francis is gone," Mackenzie said. "He took off some time last night."

John Walter swallowed two or three mouthfuls before answering. "How do you know?" he asked.

"He wrote a note."

Shrugging, John Walter said, "Doesn't matter. I can do as much as he can."

Mackenzie's mother returned carrying a cup and a plate, which she added to the stack of dishes on the counter. She ladled hot water into a dishpan and added a few flakes of washing powder. Swishing her fingers in the pan, she pointed with an elbow and said, "The tea towels are hanging on that hook. Between the two of you, you'll know where everything goes."

"Where's Ruth?" John Walter said. "This is her job."

"She's helping out a lady," Mackenzie's mother said. "I don't know her name. They're spending the morning picking berries and then canning in the afternoon."

"Mrs. Slipper," John Walter said. "She makes good jam. She's always trying to give us food." Putting down a cup, he said, "I have to use the toilet."

Mackenzie took a towel, dried one of the glasses, and placed it in the cupboard. Reaching for another one, he stopped abruptly and let the glass clunk onto the counter. He'd been tricked.

"Oh, no, you don't," he muttered. To his mother he said, "I'll be right back."

From the stoop outside the door, Mackenzie spotted his cousin making a beeline for the road. "Wait!" he called. "Where are you going?"

John Walter didn't stop.

"To Alfred's, right?" Mackenzie said. "What about me? You're supposed to take me."

John Walter looked back, puzzled. "What are you talking about?"

"Your mother said you had to do things with me," Mackenzie said.

His shoulders sagging, John Walter turned back to the house. When he reached the steps, Mackenzie tossed him the towel.

"Do you know how to get to the valley?" he asked. "That's where I want to go first."

MACKENZIE SLOWLY LOWERED HIMSELF into his uncle's rickety chair that sat alone at the corner of the house. Shifting from side to side, he felt the legs jiggle, but the nails holding it together didn't budge. Leaning back, he let his shoulders rest against the wall.

From here, Mackenzie could catch John Walter when he left the house. He smiled. It felt odd to depend on this little kid. In Bellevue, his youngest cousin had always tried to tag along with Francis and Mackenzie, even when his little legs wouldn't get him over the boulders and up the hillside they were climbing. What's he going to show me? Mackenzie wondered. Nothing like the old mine I saw yesterday.

Letting his eyes wander to the neighbouring houses, Mackenzie realized that all the homes were not identical. Like Uncle Jimmy, many of the other miners had added touches of paint to set their houses apart.

On the closest house, the one on the other side of Aunt Betsy's large garden, flowers with short green stems and large, lush petals – yellow, orange, red and purple – were painted in a bright row across the bottoms of the walls.

"Okay," John Walter called from the stoop. Jumping from the steps, he set off on a footpath that cut its way through empty lots to a dirt road. Following that street took them over the railway spur line that led to the Galt Number Three Mine, and then to the steep road down into the canyon.

"What a cracker," John Walter said.

"Who?" asked Mackenzie.

"Francis. He could've just done what Father wanted," John Walter said. "Just until Father gets better. He didn't have to run away."

Is that why Uncle Jimmy's upset? Mackenzie wondered. "What *did* your father want?" he asked.

"And why would he want to take you into the valley?" John Walter complained, ignoring Mackenzie's question. "There're plenty more good things to do in town."

"Like what?"

"Galt Park," John Walter said. "Everyone goes there. It's right by the station. The new trolley stops there. Alfred and I know how to get a ride without paying. We could show you."

"How much does it cost?" Mackenzie asked. Did his cousin really not pay?

"Or Henderson Park," John Walter said, ignoring Mackenzie again. "It's like a wild prairie on the other side of the city. There's a lake for swimming. Well, it's really just a slough. Some old guy keeps a black bear chained up that you can see. Wouldn't you rather go there?"

"Another time maybe," Mackenzie said. "After the river valley. Where's Alfred today? I thought you two were always together."

"He's busy right now."

JUST BEFORE THE ROAD DIPPED into the valley, Mackenzie and John Walter overtook a team of two powerful black workhorses and their wagon, which was loaded with lengths of lumber, cedar shingles, and wooden kegs of nails. Their halters and hooves decorated with green and white streamers, the muscled Percherons approached the hill cautiously. Talking quietly like the drayman Henry Lavallée in Saskatoon, the teamster stood in front of his seat with his feet braced against the wagon and his hands clenching the reins. The man glanced toward Mackenzie and John Walter and waved at them to go by.

At the bottom of the hill, the boys turned off the highway and onto the web of trails that led under the High Level Bridge and along the floor of the canyon. Does John Walter know where he's going? Mackenzie wondered. Can he get us back again?

A path led them through a grove of cottonwoods and into a meadow that ended in a sandy beach on the side of a small river.

"This is the Belly," John Walter said. "Did Francis bring you here?"

"No."

"I didn't think so."

The boys tugged off their boots, dropped them beside a white driftwood log, and splashed into the river. Bending low, they scooped water over their heads before wading across the cool, knee-high channel toward a sandbar.

This is a great river, Mackenzie thought, slapping his hands on the surface of the water. He and his friends were not allowed in the big river in Saskatoon because of the dangerous currents.

Pushing through tall, skinny reeds, John Walter walked down the middle of the sandbar as it flattened into a wide island and stretched around a curve in the river. Mackenzie stayed near the shore, keeping his feet in the shallow water. Reaching his hand to the bottom, he plucked up a flat, smooth stone and slipped it into his trouser pocket.

A duck squawked and the boys spied a mother mallard sailing down the passage between the island and the riverbank, pulling in her wake six scruffy ducklings. One more tiny bird sat on the mother's back. Watching that duckling peer from side to side at the passing scenery reminded Mackenzie of his sister Nellie riding in her pram. He and John Walter followed the family as it paddled back upstream and into a clump of shore plants. A moment later, the birds disappeared.

"This is a good place to find eggs," John Walter said, crouching to draw aside a stand of cattails. "Duck eggs mostly. Goose eggs the size of your fist in the spring. Mother likes them all." Standing up, he added, "Alfred says he's found arrowheads down here, but I'm not so sure." John Walter turned back.

As they came in sight of the beach, he muttered, "I wondered if he'd show up."

An old man was sitting on the log near their boots. The man's white beard was smoothly combed over his cheeks and his white hair fell to his shoulders. A blue cap, decorated with gold braid sewed to its stiff peak, was perched on the back of his head. Looking their way, the man saluted.

"Ahoy, sailors!" he called.

"Who's that?" Mackenzie asked.

"He's a crack-brained fool," John Walter said. "Don't believe anything he says."

"Are you ready to sail, young tars? The Captain needs good hands for his crew."

"He thinks he's a ship's captain." John Walter stopped a few yards from the log. "Never mind that we're thousands of miles away from any ocean." To the man, he said, "We're not sailors. And anyway, where's your boat? Where's the *Minnow?*"

"She's safe in harbour, boys. Safe in harbour. Soon she'll be ready to sail."

"The *Minnow* is his boat?" Mackenzie asked.

"His *pretend* boat." John Walter smiled. "No one's ever seen it."

"Will you sign on, lads?" the man said. "It's a sailor's life for you."

He looks harmless, Mackenzie thought. "Where are you going in your boat?" he asked.

"East," the Captain said. "East to the mighty Saskatchewan and on to Hudson Bay."

Mackenzie imagined a map of the west. What the

Captain said was possible. The Belly joined some other rivers and became the South Saskatchewan, which flowed through Saskatoon. And that river, he knew, was deep and wide and ended up at the Bay.

The Captain lifted up the two pairs of boots. His feet, Mackenzie saw, were also bare. "No need for these when you're aboard," the man said.

Mackenzie reached for his boots and found his hand swallowed in the old man's fist. The skin looked tough and weathered, like the driftwood log, but his handshake was gentle.

Walking over the beach, the boys started down a dirt path.

"Happy sailing!" the Captain called.

"He doesn't seem so bad," Mackenzie said when the old man was out of sight. He and John Walter stopped to put on their boots.

"He might sound normal but he's not," John Walter said. "What kind of boat is he going to build that could take him all that way? He's plumb crazy."

The trails in the valley looked like a web at first. But, Mackenzie saw that, sooner or later, they all ended up at the road that climbed the hillside. I might be able to find my way around down here, he thought.

John Walter stopped when they got to the outskirts of the Number Three neighbourhood. Behind him, long clouds of dirty smoke flowed from the mine's stacks.

"Do you remember the colour of our house?" John Walter asked.

"Sure," Mackenzie said. "White with blue trim. And the one beside it has paintings of flowers on the walls."

"The Galician's house," John Walter said. "You won't have any trouble finding that one. You can tell Aunt Maude I might be home for supper."

"Where are you going?" Mackenzie asked. "Wait. Don't tell me. Alfred's."

"Yes."

"What for?"

"We have stuff to do," John Walter answered.

"Does he live in Number Three?" Mackenzie said.

"Of course. His father's a miner."

"What colour's *his* house, then? How can you tell it apart?"

"It's just white," John Walter said. "But his father plants potatoes over every inch of the yard, so you can't miss it."

Should I ask to come? Mackenzie wondered. No, he decided. What would I do with two eight-year-olds?

"Go ahead," Mackenzie said. "I know how to get home."

MACKENZIE HEARD HIS AUNT MOANING the moment he walked into the kitchen. Ruth knelt beside the open door of a cupboard, her arm reaching inside for a cooking pot. Startled by Mackenzie, she dropped the pot and it thumped on the floor. Grabbing the handle, she swung it up and let it clang onto the stovetop.

"Ruth!" Mackenzie's mother hurried out of the bedroom, her face lined with fatigue. "Your mother needs quiet, child! Can you not touch anything without sounding a cannon shot?" Turning, she asked, "Where have you been, Mackenzie? I expected you home hours ago. I can't sit with Aunt Betsy and look after Nellie and prepare the meal."

"I said I'd make supper," Ruth mumbled, dropping a wooden serving spoon into the pot.

"Where's Nellie?" Mackenzie asked.

"She's lying down for her nap," his mother said, sounding angry. "But I want you to get her when she wakes up."

"I will."

Mackenzie's mother sank heavily into a chair. "I'm sorry, you two," she said. "You're both doing what you can. I shouldn't be so cross. I'm just not cut out to be a nursemaid. I want this baby to be born and Aunt Betsy back on her feet."

"Will it be soon?" Mackenzie asked.

Bending over the stove, Ruth stopped her noise-making to listen.

"The midwife says not," Mackenzie's mother said. "Mrs. Giles doesn't know what the problem is, but Aunt Betsy is starting to swell up. I don't know how to help her. If the woman's going to be the midwife, I wish she'd stay with Betsy."

"Why can't she?" Mackenzie asked.

"There are too many babies waiting to be born in Number Three," his mother said. "Mrs. Giles says she's too busy. She doesn't know when she'll be back."

"So, there might not be either a doctor or a midwife?" Mackenzie said. "That's not very good, is it?"

"The fire's gone out," Ruth said, straightening up. The cover of the firebox cracked closed. "That's not my fault."

Mackenzie said, "I'll get it going. And I'll fill the reservoir."

"Thank you, Mackenzie," his mother said.

"Ruth," she added, "you must be exhausted. I think you should give yourself a little break. Go for a walk or something just on your own. I'll be fine."

Spinning about, Ruth strode outside.

After tossing kindling into the firebox, Mackenzie said, "I'll get more wood from the pile, too."

Expecting to see Ruth, Mackenzie was surprised to find the yard empty. The door to the outhouse hung ajar on a hook. Uncle Jimmy's chair wasn't occupied. Where would she get to so quickly? he asked himself. Jumping from the stoop, he headed to the axe stuck in a block by the woodpile.

MACKENZIE SAT ON THE STEPS with Nellie. Babbling to herself, his sister pushed a small, flat stone along her arm and then dropped it – clink – into a kitchen pot.

Picking up another stone from the pile beside Mackenzie, Nellie set it carefully on her arm.

Breathing deeply, Mackenzie caught scent of the small roast beef cooking for supper. He was glad his mother was making the meal.

John Walter appeared around the side of the house. Glancing toward Mackenzie, he pumped the well handle until water gushed onto his hands. He reached for the sliver of soap kept in a broken cup on the well cover and slathered suds onto his face and neck.

"Is my father home yet?" John Walter asked.

"Yes."

"Darn."

Lathering his hands, John Walter picked up a wooden-handled brush with short, twisted bristles and scrubbed his fingers and nails. He pumped the handle, rinsed off the soap, and dried his hands on his trousers.

"What are you looking at?" John Walter asked Mackenzie.

"You missed a smudge on your forehead," Mackenzie said. "Up here." He tapped the side of his head. "And your neck's got a black line across it, just under your chin. You need a mirror."

Grimacing, John Walter rubbed his shirtsleeve over his neck and forehead. "Better?" he asked.

Mackenzie laughed. "You look like you've been in a coal mine," he said.

"Well, I haven't," John Walter said. "It's just dirt. Alfred and I were snaring gophers. They're so jittery they'd jump at their own shadows. Must be going to rain. We had to crawl almost down a badger hole to stay out of sight."

"Do you get paid for them?" Mackenzie asked.

"Five cents a tail."

"Get any?"

"Two." John Walter tucked his shirttails back into his trousers. "Alfred kept them because we were using his wire."

THE DISHES WERE DONE. Mackenzie dried the last plate and slid it onto the stack in the cupboard. Ruth wrung out the folded cheesecloth and wiped down the table's oilcloth cover. The fire in the stove was out but there was enough warm water left in the reservoir to use for handwashing later.

"Help me with this," Mackenzie said, gripping one of the handles on the wash pan. Ruth took the other side and together they hefted the pan and, careful not to let any grey water slop onto the floor, slowly walked to the door.

Immediately, Mackenzie felt cooled, the outside air chilling the perspiration on his forehead and arms. After carefully sluicing a stream onto a row of plants, Mackenzie shook out the dishpan and they turned back to the house.

Sitting in his chair tilted against a wall, Uncle Jimmy eyed the two cousins.

"You must be muscled like Ruthie," he said to Mackenzie. "You've got more of it than shows. Skinny like her, too. You're both going to have to put on some weight."

Mackenzie smiled. This was more like what he remembered: Uncle Jimmy teasing the kids.

"No, I won't," Ruth said, grinning. "I like being skinny."

"Fetch me another cup of tea, will you, love?" Uncle Jimmy said. "And another one of your cookies."

When he was alone with his uncle, Mackenzie said, "I'm sorry you have black lung."

"Who says I have black lung?" Uncle Jimmy snorted. "I've got a bad cough, that's all. And it's getting better. No rough jags today. Hardly none, anyway. When my lungs clear, the pit boss says I'll be back with my mates."

"How soon could that be?" Mackenzie asked.

"Company doctor has to thump my chest. Sign the paper. Could be any day."

"Is it hard to wait?"

"It's a terrible feeling," Uncle Jimmy said, "when you can't do anything to help yourself." He let the chair fall forward onto all four legs. "It can be like that in the mine sometimes," he said. "Helpless. Maybe there's been a bump. Men killed or badly hurt in the blast. The ceiling of a room or entry might collapse and you're stuck there, wondering where your friends are. What's happened to them? Is there damp drifting down the tunnel toward you? Just helpless."

"Has that happened to you?" Mackenzie asked.

"More than once," Uncle Jimmy said. "Worst time was at Bellevue. That huge bump ripped right through the mine. It took a long time to find everyone afterwards. Too late for some. It was a small shift. Forty-two went in but only eleven walked out, Mackenzie. It could have gone either way for me. A rescue team found my crew before the after damp did. Then we went looking for others. That's always better than waiting."

"What's after damp?"

"Those are the gases that can come out after a bump," Uncle Jimmy said. "You can't see it and you can't smell it. But if it finds you, it'll put you to sleep." Uncle Jimmy glanced at Mackenzie. "Then," he said, "it'll kill you."

Holding a cup out to her father, Ruth returned. "Aunt Maude says its gone cold and bitter," she said. "You don't have to drink it."

"Nothing better," Uncle Jimmy said.

"She'll put on the fire and warm the kettle," Ruth said.

"No, she won't," Uncle Jimmy said. "Now off you go, the two of you. See if you're needed for anything inside. I'll guard the fort."

"He still thinks Francis is coming back," Ruth murmured on the way to the door.

"Is he?" Mackenzie asked.

"I wouldn't bet on it," Ruth said. "Not anytime soon." Taking a folded cloth from the pocket of her dress, Ruth opened the layers and showed Mackenzie what looked like a piece of doughnut.

"Father's not the only one who thinks I'm too thin," she said. "Try some."

"What are those things?" Mackenzie asked, pointing to tiny flecks in the cake.

"Poppy seeds," Ruth said. "They're delicious."

Lethbridge Daily Herald

TUESDAY, AUGUST 20, 1912

MINERS STILL WAITING FOR WORK

Strike Over but Owners in No Rush to Re-open

The mineworkers' strike was finished weeks ago, but the men who toil underground are still waiting for steady shifts at the Galt collieries.

When the miners set down their tools in March of 1911, it was reported the strike would be over in a few days time. Days became weeks, weeks months, and the shutdown eventually lasted well over a year.

As the strike went on, the CPR, the biggest customer of the Galt Coal Company, found other places to buy their fuel. The miners must wait until colder weather, when their coal will be needed for heating houses and businesses.

While miners are used to the feast or famine that follows their uncertain shifts in the mines, they and their families are desperately awaiting a little of the former and an end to the latter.

CHAPTER THREE
Wednesday, August 21, 1912

Mackenzie sat in Uncle Jimmy's chair, leaning against the shady side of the house. Around the corner, he could hear his mother and Ruth sloshing laundry over a washboard. Earlier that morning, Mackenzie had hauled two tubs out of the dirt basement and into the yard. Using steel pails, he had filled the tubs, one with warm water from the stove reservoir, the other with cold rinse water from the pump.

When the washing was finished, Mackenzie could do whatever he wanted for a couple of hours. But what? he wondered. John Walter had snuck off already.

"Mackenzie!" his mother called. "We need you now."

One end of a clothesline was attached to the house, the other to the outdoor biffy. In between, the cable was held off the ground by three poles. A wicker basket holding clothespins hung from a hook on the wall.

"Help Ruth hang these whites up," Mackenzie's

mother said. "I'm going inside to check on Nellie and make sure that dinner isn't burning on the stove. When I get back, we'll do the colours. It's so hot they'll be dry in no time."

Holding a few clothespins in her mouth, Ruth reached into the rinse tub and pulled out one end of a sheet. Mackenzie slid his hands into the water. As Ruth stepped backwards, Mackenzie let the sheet trail through his fingers, and then he snagged the end before it fell. They held their arms over the tub and twisted. Smiling, Mackenzie watched water gush from the coiled cloth and then, as the sheet dried, fall from the bottom like raindrops sliding down a window. He and Ruth slipped the sheet over the line.

"Is your father around today?" Mackenzie asked as Ruth fastened the clothespins.

"He's with Mother," Ruth said. "They're talking."

Mackenzie watched his cousin tug the end of another sheet out of the tub, raising it hand over hand as the cold water drained down her arms and slid from her elbows. "Is he still angry at Francis?" he asked.

"Pick up your end," Ruth said, ignoring him. "This is getting heavy."

"I'm just curious," Mackenzie said. "How's your mother?"

Losing her grip, Ruth let the sheet splash into the tub. "Now look!" she said. Hoisting the cloth again, she twisted her end until Mackenzie felt the sheet turn in his hands. Tightening his grip, he twisted back.

When the second sheet was safely on the line, Ruth said, "Mother's getting more and more puffed up. She aches all over." Drying her hands on her apron, she said, "Mother really needs someone who knows what she's doing."

FRESHLY SCRUBBED AT THE PUMP, John Walter walked into the house in time for the noon meal. Mackenzie didn't expect him to stay, but after dinner John Walter stood at the counter with a tea towel in his hand waiting for Ruth to start the dishes.

"Do you still want to go back to the valley?" John Walter asked Mackenzie. "I could show you another way to get there."

"Sure," Mackenzie said.

When the dishes were done, John Walter led Mackenzie on a route that took them away from downtown and the highway through the valley and closer to the Galt Number Three Mine.

At the end of a dirt city street, a trail led onto a prairie meadow, fragrant with sage and littered with waist-high boulders and thorny bushes. Ahead of them, the land dropped off, tumbling out of sight down green gullies that emptied far below at the bottom of the canyon.

Stepping off the path, John Walter waved for Mackenzie to go first. He did, gladly, letting his eyes roam from the approaching gullies to a cluster of tilted concrete headstones that he thought must mark an old cemetery.

"Stop!" John Walter suddenly hissed. "Mackenzie, freeze!"

Mackenzie obeyed. Were they on the wrong path? he wondered.

"Don't move," John Walter whispered. "Don't even twitch."

"What –?"

"A rattler," John Walter said. "Didn't you hear it?"

"No." A rattlesnake! Mackenzie had never seen one before. "Where?" He felt his breath suck in. "How close?"

"It hasn't moved," John Walter said. Out of the corner of his eye, Mackenzie could see his cousin lean off to the side. "It's behind you," John Walter said. "Just off the trail."

Mackenzie was desperate to look. Was it going to bite him? "What's it doing?" He asked.

"It's not moving," John Walter said, "but it's coiled to strike. Stay still."

People die from rattlesnake bites, Mackenzie thought. Could I jump out of its reach? Am I fast enough?

"Now?" Mackenzie said.

"It's starting to uncoil," John Walter said. "Gee whiz, it's huge."

Mackenzie looked straight ahead. He didn't really want to see it. He hated snakes. Even garter snakes made him nervous. His friend Stanley in Saskatoon liked to catch garter snakes from a den behind his out-house. If it was a little one, he'd slip it inside his shirt and keep it down by his stomach for a few hours. Then, somehow, he could get the snake to slide up his chest and poke its head out from under his shirt.

"It's gone," John Walter said. "Toward the old cemetery. It's probably got a den over there."

Keeping his feet planted on the ground, Mackenzie twisted his body to look behind him. John Walter pointed to where the rattler had gone. Mackenzie turned to face his cousin.

"What did it look like?" Mackenzie asked.

"Fat," John Walter said, "with light and dark brown markings. And a big rattle on the tail. There are scads of them in this meadow. They like it in the sun. Once I saw one sleeping right on the path. You have to watch out for them all the time. They don't like being surprised – that's when they bite."

"Now you tell me," Mackenzie said. "Why did we come this way?"

"Why not?" John Walter shrugged. "It's better than the road. Not many people come this way. It's more secret."

"I can see why," Mackenzie said. "I don't want to go this way, either."

"You want to turn back?" John Walter said. "We're almost at the valley. They hardly ever go down there."

"They're in the valley?" Mackenzie remembered the day before when he and John Walter had gone barefoot.

"Not everywhere," John Walter said. "They don't cross the highway we were on. Probably afraid of getting run over."

"That's crazy to go where there are rattlesnakes," Mackenzie said. "Let's go back to the road."

"Can't," John Walter said, nodding toward the canyon. "I told Alfred I'd meet him in the bottom. He wants to look for arrowheads."

"You can count me out," Mackenzie said. "I'll find something else to do." Keeping a watch on the trail that had brought them there, he retraced his steps out of the meadow.

HALFWAY ACROSS THE OVERHEAD BRIDGE that took Ninth Street traffic up over the railway tracks and back down to First Avenue, Mackenzie stopped. Looking over the side, he rested the wooden cigar box on the bridge railing. A CPR train waited at the station, its maroon-coloured coaches glistening in the afternoon sun. A slow stream of passengers left the building and made their way along the platform to their cars.

Striding from the station to the fancy Pullman coach at the end of the train, a conductor cried, "All aboard!"

Mackenzie knew this was the same train he had arrived on. Letting his gaze sail down the line of passenger and baggage cars and past the locomotive, he followed the tracks heading west and onto the incredible High Level Bridge that spanned the canyon.

The conductor shouted his second call. Mackenzie didn't wait for the final one. Continuing over the bridge, he turned on First Avenue and followed Ruth's directions to the office of the *Daily Herald*.

Inside the building, customers formed lines on one side of a long counter. The room was alive with the hum of their voices and the constant clattering of typewriter keys. This is just like the *Daily Phoenix* office at home, Mackenzie thought. Father would fit right in. He spotted Mr. Smith typing quickly at a desk near the back. Pausing in his story, the reporter ran his fingers down his moustache. When he looked up from the paper rolled into his typewriter, he saw Mackenzie, waved, and pushed his chair away from the desk. "Hello, Mack," he called.

Mackenzie set the box on the counter and pushed it toward the reporter. "That's from my father," he said.

Mr. Smith broke the seal, opened the lid, brought the box up to his nose, inhaled deeply, and smiled. "Ah," he murmured, "your father knows a good cigar. He still doesn't smoke?" he asked Mackenzie.

"My mother won't let him."

"That, Mackenzie," Mr. Smith said, "is why I never got married. Your mother's here with you, isn't she?"

Nodding, Mackenzie said, "Yes. We're staying at my uncle's house in Number Three. My aunt's going to have a baby."

"Something I'm happy to know nothing about." Mr. Smith pulled a small paper bag from his suit pocket. "Try some of these," he said, shaking red-and-white candy balls onto the counter. "The more you suck them, the hotter they get. Take enough for your mother, too." Mr. Smith slid a newspaper off a stack and handed it to Mackenzie. "And give her my regards," he said. "Tell her to drop in when she's down-town."

"Yes, thanks," Mackenzie said.

Clutching the box in his fist, Mr. Smith returned to his typewriter.

Mackenzie made his way back to the railway station and the nearby Galt Park. A sprawling tract of flat grassland two blocks long on each side, the park seemed larger than John Walter had described. Following one of the curving pathways lined with freshly planted saplings, Mackenzie passed picnicking families and groups of chatting men enjoying the new park benches. John Walter had said there were lots of things to do here. Mackenzie couldn't see what.

At a far corner of the park, a black-and-white dog guided a team of horses and their wagon past the towering Canadian Bank of Commerce building. Customers coming and going through the bank's doors were dwarfed by four massive two-storey stone pillars. The dog barked at the horses, dashed a few feet ahead and then looked back, waiting for them to catch up. The horses never changed their pace. When they plodded closer, the dog barked at their heels again and raced off.

A clanging bell announced the arrival of a trolley car. Stopping at the corner, the uniformed driver watched a handful of passengers clamber up the two steps and into the coach. Inside, a conductor waited to collect their fares. How did John Walter and Alfred get past him without paying? Mackenzie wondered. The bell rang again, the trolley's electric motor hummed, and the bus rolled away on its steel railway tracks.

Mackenzie stepped off the curb to cross the street and then immediately stopped when he saw who was coming out of the bank. The man's blue cap was pulled down low on his forehead. His hair and beard were combed as smooth as a silk scarf. He wore a clean white sailor's tunic and dark blue trousers. The Captain set off down the sidewalk. Mackenzie ducked behind a parked motorcar to watch.

Rolling from side to side on his bow legs, the Captain touched the peak of his cap to every woman he met and saluted the men he passed. Mackenzie stepped from behind the automobile and followed him.

After strolling along for a couple of blocks, the Captain turned into a back alley. Mackenzie sped up. When he reached the lane, he peeked around the corner. The Captain was talking to someone. Neither of the men faced Mackenzie. As he watched, the sailor reached into his pocket and counted out some bills into the other man's hand.

That's a lot of money, Mackenzie thought. How would a crazy old man get to have that much cash? And why would he give it to someone else?

The second man folded the bills and slipped the wad into his pocket. He was taller than the Captain and looked younger. When the sailor took a step backwards to leave, the second man turned. Mackenzie caught a glimpse of the man's profile and quickly jumped out of sight.

Francis! Mackenzie was sure he'd just seen his missing cousin. What was he doing with the Captain? John Walter had told Mackenzie to stay away from the crazy man. Why did Francis take all that money? It doesn't matter, Mackenzie decided. All that's important is that Francis is here. He'll tell me what happened. And we'll still have time to do things together before I go back home.

Francis is going to be very surprised, Mackenzie thought. Grinning, he stepped around the corner. The laneway was empty.

OLE SIGURDSON WAS HUNCHED over the seat of his wagon, his elbows on his knees, his chin resting on his long, skinny, cupped fingers. Behind him, he could hear one of the boys scraping his shovel into the coal that had been dumped at the mine entry. These kids might make good workers some day, he thought. But for now they're slow as the dickens.

Probably full of complaints, too.

"That's it," John Walter called. "Everything's loaded."

Twisting around, the merchant frowned down his sharp nose at the paltry mound of coal in his wagon and tugged at the red bandana tied around his neck.

"You're finished, you say?" Sigurdson said.

"Yep," John Walter replied.

"A very pitiful amount of coal," Sigurdson said.

"That's the whole pile," Alfred said. "We started yesterday and finished today. You owe us ten cents each."

"Ten cents..." the man muttered. "Then there's the small matter of paying for using my equipment."

"That's not what you told me," John Walter complained. "You didn't say anything about us paying."

"Last time I checked," Sigurdson went on, "a shovel like that cost one dollar at the company store."

John Walter looked at the battered shovel at his feet. The blade was bent and split like it had been smashed against a boulder before someone tried to hammer it flat. "These aren't new," he said.

"Every time they're used there's damage and wear and tear," Sigurdson said. "You'll need to pay rent on them. Five cents a shovel ought to do it." The merchant dug one hand into the pocket of his trousers. "Ten cents less five cents. That's a nickel for each of you." Sigurdson picked through the coins in his palm.

Looking up, he said, "Unless one of you wants to make more money. Unloading. That's the easy part."

"No!" Alfred dropped his shovel to the ground.

John Walter walked closer to the wagon seat. He's probably lying, he thought. But it's money. "How much?" he asked.

MACKENZIE WORKED THE PUMP handle up and down – squeak-squawk, squeak-squawk, squeak-squawk – until cool water burst out. He washed his hands, drank from his cupped palms, and splashed water over his head.

Uncle Jimmy sat staring into the distance with his feet planted apart and his arms crossed over his chest. Mackenzie dropped onto the ground beside him. If he waited long enough, his uncle might tell him more about being a miner.

After a few minutes of silence, Uncle Jimmy stretched out his legs and crossed his ankles. "The thing is," he said, "you never think it'll be you it happens to."

Not understanding what his uncle meant, Mackenzie kept quiet.

"You know what it does to a man," Uncle Jimmy said. "You know men who've got it. Men who used to work right beside you. But you never think: that could happen to me. You think it's only the other guy who'll turn sick, never you."

Mackenzie got it. "It's the coal dust, isn't it?" he asked. "That's what makes you cough so much."

Scowling, Uncle Jimmy looked down at Mackenzie. "I've had a darn good day today," he said. "No bad coughing to speak of."

"Why can't they get rid of the dust?" Mackenzie asked.

"Some owners do their best," Uncle Jimmy said. "They put in proper fans to suck the dust out and push the fresh air in. Others would rather cut corners and hire just one boy to look after fans all over the workings. Just waiting for a disaster. The union's always after them."

Uncle Jimmy shook his head. "It's not just the miners' lungs that need good air," he said. "If the coal dust gets too thick, there can be a terrible explosion. That's what happened at Bellevue. Too much dust in the air. The methane gas got mixed in. Something set it off and the place blew as if the entire mine had been charged with dynamite."

It seemed to Mackenzie that everything about mining was dangerous. "Why did you become a miner?" he asked.

Uncle Jimmy didn't answer right away. "I never thought there was a 'why,'" he said. "Or even an 'if.' For me it was just 'when.' When can I start in the mine? My father was a miner. His father before him. And my great-grandfather, too. I couldn't wait to go underground."

"How old were you?" Mackenzie asked.

Uncle Jimmy chuckled. It was the first time Mackenzie had heard his uncle laugh this entire visit.

"Depends on who you ask," Uncle Jimmy said. "You had to be sixteen to work in the mines. I decided fifteen was old enough for me. The pit boss wanted to see a birth certificate. The only copy was at the church so that meant a trip to see the priest. I concocted a story about how there had been a mistake about the year I was born. He knew full well how old I was and why I was lying to him. But I knew other lads who had got a small change in their certificate. I knew what was needed."

"What was that?" Mackenzie asked.

"A little wink, man-to-man," Uncle Jimmy replied. "A promise I'd start regular attendance to confession. And a small bottle left in the refectory porch."

"Did you keep your promise?"

"That's none of your business," Uncle Jimmy said, grinning. "But you know, coal was king in Cape Breton in those days, Mackenzie. Being a miner was a grand job. I don't regret wanting to be a miner." He paused for a moment. "Even if I didn't really know what I was getting myself into."

The words were barely spoken when Uncle Jimmy was gripped by a bout of sharp, rasping coughs. Studying the ground by his feet, Mackenzie tried to pretend he couldn't hear his uncle. But after a few seconds, Mackenzie jumped up and dashed to the kitchen for a glass he could fill at the pump.

Snapping a large ripe tomato from its vine, Ruth marched through the garden, across the yard, up the steps, and into the kitchen. In her other hand, she clasped a package wrapped in brown butcher's paper. Mackenzie sat on the floor, bent over Nellie and a collection of pots and cutlery.

Setting the parcel on the counter, Ruth undid a circle of white string and unwrapped the paper. With her back to Mackenzie, she dribbled a handful of thumb-sized pieces of meat into a pot simmering on the stove. Chopping the tomato into small pieces, Ruth added it to the mix as well.

The smell of fresh game floated across the kitchen. Mackenzie inhaled. He guessed it might be rabbit.

Ruth wiped the butcher paper clean with the cheesecloth rag, folded the paper, and added it to that already stored in a cupboard. She wound the string around a ball and tucked it back in a drawer.

Pulling a sheet of biscuits from the stove, Ruth spilled rows of the rock-hard clamshells onto the counter to cool.

"Where have you been?" Mackenzie asked.

"Visiting," Ruth said. "Mrs. Slipper might give us some more jam."

Sprawled on his back in the bed of the wagon, John Walter slid across the pile of coal with each bump in the road. From his view over the tailgate, John Walter knew Sigurdson had steered them up the highway, out of the valley, and then to the outskirts of town, where the streets ended on the brink of the coulees.

"Steady, girl," the merchant said, shaking his horse's reins. "Down we go." Turning off a dirt road, the wagon jostled into a rutted trail that disappeared over the hill. Sigurdson clicked his tongue. "Slow and steady," he said.

Sitting up, John Walter could see they were heading down a steep hillside on a path that led to a ramshackle white building. Built into the side of the hill, the structure's steel stovepipe thrust ten feet above the roof and blew out a stream of grey and white smoke. Cables, strung from the back of the building to posts standing nearby, held rows of white sheets.

Still calling to his horse, Sigurdson guided the wagon to the side of the building. A door swung open and a Chinese man appeared wearing a long white apron. Sigurdson whistled and pulled on the reins. "Whoa!"

Climbing onto a rear wheel of the wagon, the man picked up a piece of coal. Ignoring John Walter, the man rapped the coal against the side of the wagon, held it up to look closely, and sniffed it. He repeated that with three or four chunks and then jumped down.

"Bad coal," the man said. "Too soft."

"Same as last time," the merchant said. "It was good enough for you then."

"Very bad coal," the man said. "Stinky like old eggs."

"You don't want it, I can sell it somewhere else."

"No good."

"Four dollars for the load," Sigurdson said. "Same as before."

"Two dollars!" the Chinese man cried. "No more."

"Three seventy-five." Sigurdson twisted in his seat to look at John Walter. "Get up," he said. "Get that shovel working." To the man from the laundry he said, "You won't find a better price."

"Two dollars fifty," the Chinese man countered. "Bad coal. It will burn too fast."

Shaking his head, Sigurdson flapped the reins on the horse's back and began to click his tongue. His horse swung her head around as if to see if he really meant it.

"Three dollars, okay," the Chinese man said.

What a cheat, John Walter thought. Sigurdson is paying me peanuts to load and unload his wagon. He's making heaps of money and not lifting a finger. Through an open doorway, John Walter looked into the laundry. Two large wooden-sided washtubs sat on the floor, each with a crank that tumbled the laundry through the soapy water inside. From the firebox of a hulking boiler, the rotten smell of cheap coal spewed through the room and out the door.

The Chinese man gripped a wooden cover and lifted it from a hole in the wall that opened into the building.

"Everything goes in there," Sigurdson said, jumping down from his seat.

John Walter slid his shovel into the pile on the wagon, hefted it, and tossed the coal through the hole. Shifting his feet to get his balance, John Walter heaved another shovelful off the wagon.

I'll never make enough money doing this, John Walter thought. A few coppers is all I'll get. I'm going to have to find some other job.

THE SKY OUTSIDE the bedroom window was overcast, hiding any light from the moon or the stars. Earlier in the evening, a rush of spattering rain had swooped over the yard, pelting Mackenzie with big raindrops and forcing him off his uncle's chair and into the house. The storm hadn't lasted long. By bedtime, the soil had sucked up the new moisture. Gusts of wind again raised scuds of dust on the dirt streets of the Number Three neighbourhood.

A few feet from Mackenzie, John Walter slept soundly, curled up in Francis's bed, the one he had claimed after his older brother left. It had been dark when John Walker had dragged himself through the door and wolfed down two bowls of cold leftover stew and a handful of tough biscuits. He was filthy, again. You didn't get like that, Mackenzie knew, from chasing gophers. But no one else seemed to notice. John Walter moaned in his sleep. What was he doing, Mackenzie wanted to know, that made him so tired and dirty?

Mackenzie sat up in bed. From the shadows of the neighbour's yard, a dark ball bounced toward Aunt Betsy's garden. The rabbit hesitated and then bounded between two rows. "Be careful," Mackenzie whispered.

Francis had still not come home. Was it really him that I saw? Mackenzie wondered. Maybe I was wrong. But if Francis *was* in town, where could he be hiding? Mackenzie had no idea where to look. Flopping back on the bed, he wished he knew more about Lethbridge.

Lethbridge Daily Herald

WEDNESDAY, AUGUST 21, 1912

CPR HARVEST EXCURSION TRAIN HAS LEFT HALIFAX

Tens of Thousands Will Arrive in West

Another CPR harvest excursion train has departed Halifax to begin its journey west. Last year, over 30,000 men boarded trains in the Maritimes, Quebec or Ontario and it is expected just as many will join the expedition this summer.

As the travellers try to get comfortable in the crowded second-class cars, they will be thinking of the grand wages that await them, perhaps as much as $300.00 for a short stay on the farm. All along the CPR main line, agents are awaiting the arrival of this train. Once they debark, the easterners will be taken to a farm where they will hope to find at least a clean and not overly crowded shelter.

Each year, when this work is complete, many harvesters feel the Call of the West and buy homestead land from the CPR. It is expected hundreds will find the promise of their own farm irresistible again this year.

CHAPTER FOUR
Thursday, August 22, 1912

After folding the *Lethbridge Daily Herald* to an inside page, Mackenzie's mother lay the newspaper on the kitchen table. "This is yesterday's edition," she told Mackenzie. "Did you read the article about the harvest excursion?"

"No," Mackenzie said, carefully drawing one of Aunt Betsy's knives down a rough sharpening stone, first with the cutting edge dangerously facing his thumb, then facing away. "Sixteen, seventeen, eighteen..." When he had counted twenty times on each side, he set the knife on the counter and picked up another.

"Go read it to Aunt Betsy," his mother said. "Leave the knives."

Skimming over the beginning of the article, Mackenzie asked, "Why?"

"Just read it," his mother said. "It'll give her a chuckle."

"Does she *want* me in there?"

"Yes! Now get going."

Mackenzie knocked softly on Aunt Betsy's door and entered when she called. His aunt's eyes were closed. Her face was pale, and glistening with a film of perspiration.

"Mother wants me to read something to you," Mackenzie said.

Frowning, Aunt Betsy opened her eyes and focused on Mackenzie. "I've a terrible headache," she said. "Maybe this will take my mind off it."

As Mackenzie read from the newspaper, Aunt Betsy began to smile.

"That's how we met, Jimmy and me," she said when Mackenzie finished. "Did you know that, Mackenzie? Jimmy was one of the men who caught the harvest excursion in Halifax. He was a young man then. He bought a ticket going west, to Regina, to make a little fortune on the harvest, he said, and then to look for work in the mines. His father was a Cape Breton miner, and down East they'd heard only good things about the mountain mines. The big rooms. The newest equipment."

Aunt Betsy waved her fingers. Mackenzie stepped closer and raised a glass of water to her lips.

"The men were crowded into old CPR coaches so badly, some slept in the luggage racks," she went on. "They packed a little food but it didn't last. It took five days just to get to Winnipeg.

"When the train stopped to take on coal and water, all the men raced into the station. Jimmy walked outside where some families had set up a little market to sell things from their gardens."

Aunt Betsy laughed. "I was working there with your Aunt Bernice, Mackenzie. I caught his eye right away, so he says. He bought a bundle of carrots from us and we chatted away until the all aboard. Then he ran back to the train, grabbed his bag, and jumped off before it got up speed."

"He never helped on the harvest?" Mackenzie asked.

"He hired on a few times around Winnipeg," Aunt Betsy said, "but he was never happy doing it. He hated the grain dust. Made him feel itchy all the time. And one of the farms he went to had snakes. Hundreds of them twisting all over each other in a rock pit. They liked to hide in the stooks of grain he had to throw onto the wagon. Frightened Jimmy half to death." Aunt Betsy gently shook her head. "All of my big, strong men are scared of snakes, father and sons," she said.

"Five months later we were married and he was working in the Bellevue mine. Your grandparents weren't too pleased to have him steal me away, you can imagine. They grew to love him, though." Aunt Betsy waved for more water.

"What did you think about moving to a little town in Alberta?" Mackenzie asked.

"Oh!" Aunt Betsy cried. "I was in love. I didn't care

where we lived." Slowly her face darkened. "There was one thing I didn't like," she said. "The Galicians. In the city, there were all kinds of different people, but everyone lived in their own neighbourhoods. There was no mixing, so we didn't have to see how poorly the peasants from Europe lived. That's not what it was like in the mining towns. We were all thrown together like vegetables into a stew pot. A person was as likely to speak some foreign language to you as they were English. It's getting like that in Number Three too. I don't like it."

"What do you mean?" Mackenzie asked. He'd heard other people talk like that about Galicians, but never anyone in his own family.

"When we first moved here from Bellevue, everyone spoke English," his aunt said. "But that's all changed. A woman lives beside us now who hardly knows a word."

The Galicians' house, Mackenzie thought. The one with the painted flowers. "Have they done something to you?" he asked.

"Oh, Mackenzie," Aunt Betsy said. "Don't start like that. You sound like Jimmy getting after me and I'm too sick to explain myself." She took a sip of water and then smiled.

"Do you know who really liked that story about Jimmy and me when he was a boy?" Aunt Betsy's voice had become cheerful again. "Wanted to hear it over and over? Francis."

"He did?"

"Said it was like an unfinished fairy tale. It starts with Jimmy setting out to make his fortune. In the middle he meets his true love. But it doesn't have its ending, yet. Francis says working in a coal mine is no way to finish a fairy tale."

"Aunt Betsy?" Mackenzie said. "Where do *you* think Francis is?"

Aunt Betsy fixed her gaze on Mackenzie.

"I miss him," Mackenzie said. "I thought we'd have time to do things together."

"I miss him, too, Mackenzie," Aunt Betsy said. "I have a feeling he's not far away. And soon he'll let us know what he's up to. He might even be persuaded to come back."

That settles it, Mackenzie thought. I'm tracking him down.

"Put the glass back on my dresser, please, Mackenzie," Aunt Betsy said, closing her eyes. "I'll catch a little sleep before this boy starts kicking again."

As soon as he'd finished sharpening all of the knives, Mackenzie filled the kitchen water jug and the stove reservoir. He chopped kindling and filled the wood box. Then, like John Walter had done hours before, he snuck out of the house.

Making a beeline for the road, Mackenzie turned his back on the rumbling boilers of the Galt Number

Three Mine and started toward the Ninth Street Overhead Bridge and downtown. When he reached Galt Park, Mackenzie followed the paths to get to the Bank of Commerce building. From there, he could follow the Captain's route to the only place he'd seen Francis. Turning into the laneway, he saw that the backs of the buildings made a wall down each side of the alley. Francis and the Captain had disappeared so quickly, Mackenzie decided, they must have gone through a door into one of these stores.

Near the far end of the alley, a team of horses stood harnessed to a wagon. The cart's short, wooden sides were stained black. In the bed, a man wearing a red bandana shuffled his feet to get a hold in the loose chunks of coal. Pushing a shovel into the load, the man heaved the coal into a hole, where it rattled down a steel chute into a basement. The man stopped after every three or four shovelfuls to wipe a blackened sleeve over his sweaty forehead, once glancing toward Mackenzie standing alone at his end of the alley.

Making his way to where Francis had been standing, Mackenzie found a door labelled Finch Hardware. Returning to the street, he peered in the front windows. On the other side of displays of carpentry tools, the room was lined with shelves holding all sorts of barrels and boxes along with rifles and shotguns hanging from wires attached to the ceiling. It's like Douglas Hardware at home, Mackenzie thought, stuffed to the rafters. He stepped inside.

Walking slowly toward the back of the store, he found every aisle empty.

Following the sound of voices, Mackenzie found two clerks wearing dark green aprons. The men, one with grey hair, the other not much older than Francis, were bent over a catalogue spread open on a counter.

The older man looked up as Mackenzie approached. "What are you after, lad?" he asked.

"I'm looking for Francis," Mackenzie said.

"Who's he?" the clerk asked.

"My cousin."

Frowning, the younger man straightened up, bracing his hands on the countertop. "Can't you see Mr. Finch is busy?" he said. "Don't come in here just to waste his time."

"It's no bother, James," Mr. Finch said. "What happened to your cousin? You lose him?"

"Sort of," Mackenzie said. "I saw him yesterday in the lane beside your back door. Then he disappeared. I think he might have come in here."

"Hundreds of people come in here every day," James said. "How would we know which one is your cousin?"

"He was with the Captain," Mackenzie said.

"Him!" the older man said. "Do you know who that is, James?"

"Everyone does," the younger clerk said. "He's that old coot who lives by himself in some cave in the valley. Calls himself a riverboat captain. He's a bit cracked."

"He was here, all right," Mr. Finch said, turning to Mackenzie. "And there was a young fellow with him. I remember thinking they were a strange pair. The lad was spending the money, but the supplies seemed to be for the old goat."

"What sort of supplies?" Mackenzie asked.

"Well," Mr. Finch said, scratching his head. "Let me think."

"I cut him thirty feet of rope," James said.

"We'd just got some canvas in," Mr. Finch said. "He took a nice ten-foot square. A pound of nails..."

"After I bound the ends of the rope," James said, "I had to go back into the storeroom for a shovel."

"What was your cousin doing with the old boy, anyway?" Mr. Finch asked.

"I don't know," Mackenzie said.

"The Captain comes in here fairly often," Mr. Finch said, "for one thing or another. He's usually got someone in tow, someone he's convinced to give him a hand with whatever he's up to. Likely that's what was going on yesterday." He scratched his head. "The last I saw him, the Captain was grinning and heading out the door with his armload of goods."

Pointing to a page in the catalogue in front of him, Mr. Finch said to James, "Get your pencil out again. We've got more work to do." He tapped his finger on the counter. "I want you to add to that list."

Left to wonder what had happened to his cousin, Mackenzie found his way out of the hardware store.

AGED A DIRTY GREY, CRACKED and splintered by years of weather, the door was thrown open to expose the first braces of a mineshaft that lead into the hillside. Long ago the steel tracks and wooden ties had been torn from the mine's floor.

John Walter dropped a bundle of clothing on the ground and stepped into the entrance. He was met with a surge of cold, musty air, as if the mine had been waiting to release its stale breath. He shivered. John Walter heard running water trickling down the shaft toward the entrance. Groping along the ground, he found a board about a yard long and a foot wide. Holding it up to the light from outside, John Walter saw the piece of wood was caked with dry dirt. There were words under the dirt, but the only ones he could read were, "Mine," and "Stay Out!"

Dropping the sign against the wall, he spotted what he was looking for. He returned to Alfred holding in each hand a tarnished lantern, the top half covered with a fine steel mesh and the bottom with a glass chimney.

"We're supposed to use those?" Alfred asked. "Those're Wolf lamps. They're what my grandfather used. They don't put off enough light to even see a couple of yards. We should have carbide lamps." He tapped his head. "In our caps. Like real miners."

"Sorry," John Walter said. "Sigurdson said this is all he's got."

"Do they have fuel?" Alfred asked.

"They'll be good for a few hours," John Walter said. "If we leave them here when we're done for the day, he'll fill them again. I've got a flint."

"Where are the tools?" Alfred asked.

"Inside," John Walter said, "at the face."

"They'd better not be like those shovels." Alfred shook out a pair of old trousers, a threadbare shirt, some well-darned socks and a blackened, paper-thin cap. Dropping his regular clothes on the ground, he pulled on the mine clothes.

"I brought water," Alfred said, holding up a battered copper canteen. "And food," he added, shaking a tin container with the word, "Dynamite," stamped on the lid.

"I can guess what that is," John Walter said, at the sound of things thumping inside the container. Kneeling over one of the lamps, he struck his flint to light the flames. The boys headed inside, feeling the ground rise slowly under their feet as they climbed into the mine.

"Is this even Sigurdson's place?" Alfred asked.

"Depends how you mean," John Walter said. "If you mean does he own it, no. But he uses it."

"Whose is it, then?"

Shrugging, John Walter said, "Maybe nobody's, it's so old."

As the sunlight at their backs dimmed, the lanterns gradually seemed to brighten the cavern like the moon shining through a cloudy sky. Passing a small tunnel that branched off from the entry, they turned down a second shaft that soon opened into a room. The light from the lamps dampened as it spread across the open space toward the black walls and over a wooden barrow with a steel-rimmed wheel.

Looking around the room, John Walter spied a coal seam no more than two feet high at the bottom of a wall. Propped close by were a pickaxe and a short-handled shovel.

"Right where Sigurdson said they'd be." John Walter hefted the pick and poked the tip into the coal. "Whoever mined this room must've decided it wasn't worth messing with that little seam."

"Maybe they didn't feel like laying down to get at it." Alfred picked up the shovel. "We're not giving him a cent for these old things," he said, knocking the blade against the rock wall. "He's not going to cheat us out of our pay again."

"I told him," John Walter said. "I told him he has to pay us full wages." He swung the tip of the pick at the band of coal. A chunk about the size of a loaf of bread dropped to the floor with a muffled thud.

Resting the axe head on the floor, John Walter spit on the palms of his hands and rubbed them together. "Come on, Alfred," he said. "We're miners now. Get that shovel and start filling our barrow."

BUILT WITH DIRT AND ROCKS and hundreds of wagonloads of cinders dumped from locomotives, the steep-sided embankment carried the railway tracks from the station to the beginning of the High Level Bridge. From here, Mackenzie could see over the highway that led into the valley, past the cemetery and the snake-infested meadow, and beyond the dirty smokestacks at the Galt Number Three Mine.

He could also read the sign nailed to the post standing in front of him. "No Trespassing," it said. "Stay Off Bridge."

Mackenzie looked past the sign to follow the pair of steel rails that joined into one and stretched forever across the valley. From the middle, Francis had said, you can see for miles down the canyon. Everything is visible. Was he telling me something? Mackenzie wondered. Balancing both feet on a rail, he started down the tracks toward the bridge.

IT WASN'T SCARY, he quickly decided. A floor under the tracks blocked his view straight down and made it impossible to tell how high he was. Four-foot walls stopped him from seeing much over the sides. The bridge was so long; he knew he would catch any train coming when it was still far away. Slipping off the rail, he walked awkwardly on the ties. Stepping on every second timber was a bit short for his legs, and every third was a bit far.

When he guessed he was halfway across, Mackenzie stopped. He'd been walking for about ten minutes.

Resting his chin on top of a wall, Mackenzie saw the valley spread out underneath him. From this height, the sides of the canyon were sandy brown and yellow, with a little green growth in the gullies and on the shores of the Belly River. Going up on tiptoes, Mackenzie looked straight down to the bottoms of the steel towers. Francis had told him the bridge was as high as thirty houses stacked one on top of another. The bridges in Saskatoon were only five or six stories high.

Mackenzie started to feel light-headed, as if a wind was trying to pull him over the wall. He dropped back onto his feet and stepped into the middle of the bridge until the wooziness passed.

When he felt ready, Mackenzie peered down at the shiny blue water of the Belly River. Following its course between banks of sand and drifting beds of gravel, the Belly looked no bigger than a creek.

A few hundred yards downriver, a man worked in the shade of some shoreline cottonwood trees, hammering nails into long, wooden planks. Smiling, Mackenzie watched as the man swung his arm down to the board. Mackenzie waited for the sound of the sharp crack of the hammer to reach him. Near the man, more boards, a heap of boxes, and an assortment of cloth bags were visible in the mouth of a grey canvas tent.

The man's white hair and beard were unmistakable. Studying the campsite, Mackenzie tried to figure out what else the man had gathered. Looking deeper under the trees, he spied what looked like a pile of about a dozen logs, each ten feet long and skinned clean of its bark.

The Captain's getting ready, Mackenzie decided. He's building his ship. Studying the river and nearby valley, Mackenzie searched for a landmark to use when he tried to find the Captain's worksite. I'm going there, he told himself. He'll have to tell me where Francis went.

The timbers under his feet began to vibrate. Shooting a glance to the far side of the valley, it took a few moments for what he saw to sink in. He wasn't alone on the bridge. A black locomotive was rumbling toward him, churning smoke over the dull red freight cars it pulled behind.

"Shoot!" Mackenzie muttered. He'd have to get out of the way. With a half-mile head start, he knew the freight train wasn't going to catch him. Other trains he'd seen crossing the bridge all moved very slowly.

This slowly? Mackenzie wondered, stepping on every other tie. Maybe he should run a bit. He tried, but it was hard getting his stride to match the ties. Whenever a foot dropped between the timbers, his toe caught and he stumbled and almost fell.

Mackenzie looked over his shoulder. The train was getting closer. He ran again, but trying to keep his feet on the ties, he wasn't going very fast. If the engineer saw him, would he stop?

Francis had told him workers had been killed building the bridge. More people had died once it was completed. Some of them fell or jumped. Others had been struck by a train. It was stupid of me to come up here, Mackenzie thought.

The locomotive was gaining on him, he could see, and Mackenzie was still a long way from the end. Would there be enough room for the train to get past if he pressed himself against the wall? It didn't look like it. He ran quicker, tripped, got his balance, and kept going.

Why wasn't the engineer putting on the brakes? Mackenzie could clearly make out the bars of the cattle catcher that thrust out in front of the locomotive. The engineer must to able to see him.

I have go faster, he thought. Mackenzie stretched his stride to cover four ties. Now he was moving! He felt like an antelope bounding across the prairie. Leap! Leap! Leap!

Mackenzie felt his right foot slide. He lost his thrust and his left foot dropped between two ties. Before he could set his right foot again, the toes of his left caught on a tie and jerked him down like a lassoed steer. Mackenzie fell, his hands and shoulder striking wood, his tangled legs trapped between timbers. Wracked by pain that jolted his body, Mackenzie cringed at the angry blast of the locomotive's whistle.

JOHN WALTER AND ALFRED sat just outside the entrance to the mine, their backs against a boulder, their faces warmed by the sun's glare as it appeared over the top of the valley. Tilting his head back, Alfred took a long swallow from his canteen and then passed it to John Walter. Wiping the back of his hand over his forehead, Alfred frowned at the black dust and then adjusted his cap.

"It'd be easier working in there with a carbide lamp," Alfred said.

"You're right," John Walter said. "When we get more coal dug, we'll have enough money to buy our own. Not like Sigurdson's junk, either. Everything'll be store-bought."

"How long do you think it will take to fill Sigurdson's wagon again?" Alfred asked. "There's not much left in that seam we've been working at."

"It's pathetic," John Walter said. "We'll find a better one." Pushing himself to his feet, he said, "You wait. We'll have a good load ready by tomorrow. Our first big pay."

FIRMLY CLUTCHING THE LITTLE wooden box in her hand, Ruth hurried across the yard and stopped at the bottom of the steps. Opening her fingers, she admired the delicate paintings on the sides of the container. She lifted the lid and rustled the dry leaves inside with her fingertips. The fragrance that rose from the box reminded her of the dry prairie.

The leaves were from a raspberry plant that hung from the rafters of the woman's back porch. Ruth's directions were simple: brew a strong tea with the leaves every few hours and make sure her mother drinks it.

Replacing the lid, Ruth held the box to her chest and went inside the house. Seeing the kitchen was empty, she opened a cupboard and pushed the box out of sight behind a mason jar. Ruth rekindled the fire under the kettle and went into her mother's bedroom.

MACKENZIE SCRAMBLED TO HIS FEET. His hands stung. His shoulder ached. His legs felt bruised but they held him up. He didn't have to look to know how close the locomotive was. He could hear the boiler chuffing. The shrill squawk of the locomotive's brakes – tons of steel sliding over the rails hammered into the bridge – screamed into his ears. Hopping onto a railway tie to get his balance, he sprinted away.

Behind him, it sounded like the train cars were slamming into each other, the whole line battering against the locomotive. The train was stopping. Mackenzie risked a look over his shoulder. Two men, leaning out each side of the locomotive, were shaking their fists at him.

"Hey, you, kid!" The angry voice caught Mackenzie

near the end of the bridge. "If I get my hands on you..."
Was anyone chasing him?

Not yet. Mackenzie didn't slow down. If there was someone watching from the station or if the men in the CPR shops heard the train suddenly stop, they might try to grab him. Jogging off the bridge, he slid on his feet and backside down the embankment to the ground. Getting his feet under him, he scrambled toward the edge of the canyon, log-rolled under the end of the bridge, and lay panting to catch his breath.

Sitting up, Mackenzie studied his injuries. He had a few bloody scrapes. The sleeve of his shirt was torn. His skin was already bruising. If he washed in the river, he'd be good as new. And who would notice at his aunt's house, anyway?

LATER THAT AFTERNOON, with his hands hidden in his pockets, Mackenzie approached his uncle. When he reached the corner, Mackenzie slid down the wall until his seat was on the ground and his elbows rested on his knees.

"It's not the same thing, I know," Uncle Jimmy said after Mackenzie was settled. "It's not like losing your life to a bump. But it's darn hard when you and your comrades decide you have to walk away from the mine. You have to lay down your tools and turn your back on your job and any hope of a wage. That's a miserable thing to do."

"A strike?" Mackenzie asked.

"Twice in five years," Uncle Jimmy said. "The first time in '06. The union was new and the mineworkers struck all through the Crowsnest Pass. Shut down everything. Not a pound of coal came out of the mines. All we wanted were a few more pennies from the owners' profits so we could feed our families and put a stop to the conditions that were killing our mates.

"They came down on us hard, Mackenzie. Hired goons to attack us when we tried to have a meeting. Bombed houses. Roughed us up when we marched on the mine. Miners – and their wives, too – got the brunt of their thuggery."

"Women got beaten up?" Mackenzie asked.

"They didn't back down," Uncle Jimmy said.

"Aunt Betsy?"

Mackenzie saw his uncle smile. "Don't you tell your grandparents," Uncle Jimmy said. "Betsy's never let on what happened. They wouldn't have thought too much of their daughter being part of that. She was raised to not make a fuss."

Holding his fist against his lips, Uncle Jimmy took a slow breath and then let the air rumble from his chest. He reached down for a cup near his chair and took a sip of water.

"And scabs," Uncle Jimmy went on. "They brought in scabs. Out-of-work know-nothings from south of the border. Farmers looking for some extra money. The owners took them into the mines and gave them our jobs," he said. "No mind they made such a mess of things it took years to clean up behind them."

"What did you do then?" Mackenzie asked.

"Got stronger," Uncle Jimmy said. "Stood shoulder to shoulder to try to keep the scabs out. Got knocked about a bit more. We never broke. We came from all over, Mackenzie, to work in those mines. Cape Breton. Wigan. Appalachia. Galicia. Sometimes you couldn't understand what the next man was saying. But it was all for one and one for all right to the end."

"Did you get what you wanted?" Mackenzie asked.

"A pittance." Uncle Jimmy spat. "Nothing more than a pittance. We never made back what we'd lost going out. Contract miners like me – those who get paid for how much coal we bring out, not how many hours we work – we had a hard time making ten dollars a day. Each year after we went back it got worse again, until last year when we struck in the spring."

"Did they bring in scabs again?"

"Hah!" Uncle Jimmy cried. "No, they didn't, bless them. This time it suited the owners to close down the mines altogether. They had no need for scabs anymore than they needed us because there was no one who wanted to buy their coal. They kept us out for over a year, long after we were desperate to get our jobs back."

Uncle Jimmy pulled a watch from his trouser pocket. "Quitting time," he said. "I can almost hear the boys laying down their tools and making their way to the lift. On a good day, after we'd hung up our wet clothes and washed, we'd have a cup of tea before coming home. I should be down there with them, Mackenzie."

Pushing himself to his feet, Mackenzie said, "I'll get you some tea, Uncle Jimmy. Ruth made a pot. You wait here."

A minute later, Mackenzie returned with a cup. "I didn't put anything in it. Just the way you like it."

Nodding his thanks, Uncle Jimmy took a long drink, got a surprised look on his face, and spit the mouthful onto the ground. "What have you given me?" he cried.

"Tea."

"That's no tea," Uncle Jimmy said. "It tastes like slough water."

"Aunt Betsy drank it," Mackenzie said.

Uncle Jimmy cleared his throat. "She's being fed all sorts of concoctions," he said. "That doesn't mean they'll do *me* any good."

Lethbridge Daily Herald

THURSDAY, AUGUST 22, 1912

LOCAL OWNER UPSET WITH THIEVES STEALING FROM HIS MINE

Robbers Selling Coal to Unsuspecting Buyers

At least one owner of a small coal mine near the outskirts of Lethbridge has complained to police after thieves set up their own operation in his colliery. Mr. Stevens, proprietor of the Apex Fuel and Coal Company, found evidence recently that wagonloads of his high-quality coal have been pilfered and sold.

"At this time of year, my mine is not being worked," Mr. Stevens said. "The entrance is boarded over to prevent access."

That has not been enough to stop some brazen robbers who gained entry and treated the coal inside as their own.

Mr. Stevens is also concerned that reckless or inexperienced individuals may come to serious harm inside his mine. "My mine is perfectly safe," he said, "if the men know which rooms to work in. I cannot be responsible for any thieves who blunder into danger."

CHAPTER FIVE
Friday, August 23, 1912

J ohn Walter could be dead, Mackenzie thought, the way he's laid out flat on his back. Leaning over Francis's bed, Mackenzie stared at John Walter's chest. Not a muscle moved. He poked his cousin in the ribs. Nothing. What's he been doing to make himself so tired? Mackenzie wondered.

Sitting down on the other cot, Mackenzie studied John Walter's face and his fingers which gripped the top of the sheet. Every day he looks more like Uncle Jimmy did when he came home from the mine, Mackenzie thought. Except John Walter's dirtier. He doesn't try very hard to scrub clean. Whoever sees those sheets next laundry day is going to give him the dickens.

Fluffing his pillow and pulling up the covers to make his bed, Mackenzie thought about his older cousin. It *was* Francis I saw in the alley, he thought. I got that much right. But he won't be coming home. I think I know why, too. If Uncle Jimmy would just tell me, I'd know for sure.

Did Francis know what was coming? That first day, when he showed me the mine, did he know he would be leaving home that soon?

Mackenzie decided Francis did know but he didn't want anyone else to. Not even me, thought Mackenzie. That's why he wouldn't tell me what kind of job he wanted. All he really told me was that from the High Level Bridge you could see everything in the valley. And I saw the Captain.

Mackenzie slipped on his clothes. The Captain. Francis wanted me to understand the old man knows something, he thought. Now, if the crazy coot will just tell me what it is.

RUTH SAT ALONE IN THE KITCHEN, softly tapping a small glass bottle against the tabletop. Mackenzie lifted the lid on the porridge pot, spooned some oatmeal into one of the three bowls on the counter, and joined his cousin.

"What's that?" he asked.

Ruth slid the bottle toward him. "For Mother," she said.

Unscrewing the lid, Mackenzie raised the bottle to smell the clear liquid inside.

"Nothing," he said, and sniffed again.

Replacing the lid, Mackenzie shook the bottle until frothy bubbles appeared.

"What is it?" he repeated.

"Castor oil," Ruth said.

"Castor oil! Isn't that what makes you run to the toilet? Why are you giving that to your mother?"

Ruth reached across the table and retrieved the bottle. "It's supposed to help the baby come," she said.

"Who says?" Mackenzie asked. He hadn't heard anything about Mrs. Giles, the midwife, being here.

"Mother's really sick," Ruth said. "She's swollen up all over. Everything aches. Nothing's working."

"What are you going to do?"

"Me?" Ruth said. "How am I supposed to know what to do?"

"What about Uncle Jimmy?"

"Have you seen him?" Ruth said. "All he can think about is his old job. He hardly knows Mother's expecting. She said it was the same with us, too. He always found some reason to leave just as a baby was about to be born. It'll probably be no different this time."

"I'll talk to my mother," Mackenzie said. "She must have an idea."

"Go ahead," Ruth said. "But she'll just say she wants to get a doctor and Mother will just say no."

"So you're going to give her the castor oil?" Mackenzie asked.

"Yes," Ruth said, "unless the baby comes out on his own."

WHEN MACKENZIE WENT BACK UPSTAIRS, John Walter's boots were gone. The bed was unmade and empty. When he returned to the kitchen, only one clean bowl remained. *How did he do that without me seeing him?* Mackenzie wondered.

"The thing is," Uncle Jimmy said a few minutes later, "when you spend half your life underground, you become part of the mine. It's not just the owner's mine. It's your mine and your comrades' mine. You don't own the colliery, but you're loyal to it. That's the only place you want to work."

Mackenzie tried to imagine what it would be like to want to work in a dark, wet place that might kill you. "Why?" he asked.

"Because you made it," Uncle Jimmy said. "It was your sweat and blood that drilled the entries and dug out the rooms. My old father used to say that a miner was proud of what he built, just like a carpenter. Except a carpenter finds an empty place and brings his lumber and nails and builds a house where there was nothing before. A miner does it differently. He takes away what he needs until he's built this big space where there was solid rock and coal before."

Uncle Jimmy stopped to clear his lungs. Mackenzie hardly noticed the coughing anymore. It was like someone with a cold stopping to sneeze. You just waited until he was finished and ready to go on.

"When you've given so much of your life to the

mine and the owners," Uncle Jimmy said, "it's a terrible surprise to know they're not so loyal to you. They can dump you as easy as a load of dirty coal."

"What happened?" Mackenzie asked.

"They called me in yesterday," Uncle Jimmy said. "The company doctor was here to give the verdict on a few of us. I'd never set eyes on him before. Some quack who does the company's bidding." Turning away, he spit into his handkerchief.

"He spent two minutes with me," Uncle Jimmy went on. "He stuck that thing on my chest to listen to me breathing. Said I was unfit. No breath. Could never work underground again, he said. Mine manager's sitting right there nodding his head. 'No more,' he says."

Uncle Jimmy stared past the garden in the direction of the Number Three Mine. Mackenzie didn't know what to say. His uncle must be really sick. "What's going to happen?" he asked.

"They'll find me some so-called job," Uncle Jimmy said. "I'll be a day man. A company man. No more contract work. Guys like me they put bone picking on the belt."

"What's that, Uncle Jimmy?" Mackenzie asked.

"Bone pickers scramble on their toes all day, picking dirt and rock from the lump coal on the belts going to the rail cars. When your legs give way, you're put to cleaning the yard. Same as when you're first hired on." Uncle Jimmy hawked and spit. "Sick miners and eager young pups doing the same thing."

"Is that how Francis would have started?" Mackenzie asked.

"All he had to do was walk through the gate," Uncle Jimmy said. "There was a job waiting for him. It was all set. A year of keeping his nose clean and he'd be underground. I'd see to that, too."

"But he refused," Mackenzie said.

Uncle Jimmy swung his head to peer at Mackenzie. Frowning, he looked like he wondered if he'd said too much.

"I won't tell anybody," Mackenzie said. Quickly, he added, "I think I'll go back to the valley today. Do you know the old guy down there who calls himself the Captain?"

"What have you got to do with him?" Uncle Jimmy asked.

"I saw him when I was with John Walter one time," Mackenzie said. He didn't think he should tell his uncle he'd also seen him with Francis. "John Walter said he was cracked. He could never be a riverboat captain."

"He's maybe not all there," Uncle Jimmy said, tapping a finger on the side of his head. "I guess for years he's been saying he's going to ship away. It's just he's always getting ready but he never leaves. The water's so low this summer, if he tried he'd probably never get any further than the first sandbar." Uncle Jimmy wiped a handkerchief across his lips. "I wouldn't want you spending time with him."

"I won't," Mackenzie said. "Where does he get his money?" Mackenzie stopped. How would I know he has money? he asked himself. "I heard he has a pile saved up in the bank."

"He works odd jobs," Uncle Jimmy said. "There are shops downtown always looking to give someone two bits to sweep the sidewalk or shovel snow. Over time those two bits would add up, I suppose."

"Do you think he really lives in a cave?" Mackenzie asked.

"A cave, a shack, a tent," Uncle Jimmy said. "He's not the only hermit who gets by down in the valley."

JOHN WALTER LAY ON HIS SIDE on the ground, one shoulder inside the trench he'd dug out at the base of the wall. Sliding the pick over the floor, he cracked the tip of it into the seam. He reached into the opening and brushed out a fist-sized lump of coal.

"Got it," Alfred said, scraping the coal onto his shovel and tossing it into the wheelbarrow. "I'll take this load out," he said, setting his Wolf lamp in the barrow. "And I'll bring us back some more water."

"Tell me how close we're getting to a wagonload," John Walter said. In the dim light of his own lamp, he watched his friend pick up the handles of the barrow and steer it out of the room. The wheel's steel rim chattered over the rocks scattered across the floor.

John Walter struck the coal seam again, twisted the

handle and heard a small piece fall to the floor. Alfred, John Walter knew, wanted to go home. He was coughing a lot in the dusty air and was always thirsty. Getting outside in the sunlight would make him feel better. John Walter couldn't quit. He was going to stay in the mine until he had enough coal to fill old Sigurdson's wagon. Tightening his grip on the axe, he swung again.

A few minutes later, John Walter stood up and tried to straighten his back to ease his aching muscles. From far down the entry, he heard the wheelbarrow crackling slowly toward him. As the noise grew louder, he knelt down, about to slide into the trench and get at more coal.

The bump struck without warning, roaring down toward the entry from deep in the hill. The walls of the tunnel wrenched sideways. Heavy supporting beams splintered like kindling. The floor heaved. A curtain of black dust fell into the room. Then the rock stopped shifting, almost before John Walter had time to tell it had begun. Stumbling, he caught his breath and sucked in a cloud of powdered coal.

Hacking to clear his lungs, John Walter spit black mud. He wiped a dirty sleeve across his mouth and spit again.

The room was completely quiet, the only sound the ringing deep inside his ears as they recovered from the blast. Through the heavy dust, John Walter spied the pickaxe near his feet. Nearby, his lamp stood untouched, the tiny wick still burning. Alfred's dynamite container hadn't toppled.

Bending down, John Walter grabbed the pickaxe handle to lift it from the floor. It wouldn't budge. He jerked the handle but it felt nailed down. It dawned on John Walter that the top of the trench he'd been digging out had collapsed down onto the floor, pinning his tool. He stumbled away from the wall. Moments before he'd been inside that trench.

Where was Alfred? John Walter remembered hearing the wheelbarrow. Alfred had been close, somewhere in the entry.

"Alfred!" His voice caught on the dust in his throat. Coughing, he called again.

No sound.

He couldn't see far through the thick dust, but the floor of the room was still flat and the braces were unbroken. Reaching for his lamp, he walked to the entry.

Part of the ceiling had collapsed onto the floor, leaving a ragged hole on top and a mound of rock and broken timbers that almost filled the tunnel. The shattered bed of the wheelbarrow was visible under the edge of the pile. Alfred's canteen was there, too, flattened like a big penny.

Alfred lay nearby, his head and shoulders exposed but the rest of his body hidden by rubble. Kneeling down, John Walter shook his friend's shoulder.

"Alfred?" he said.

Alfred didn't move as John Walter laid his hand on his cheek. Cold, John Walter thought, like a dead man.

MACKENZIE STAYED AWAY FROM the patch of prairie John Walter had led him into. From the road he was walking on, he thought he could almost see the rattlesnakes sunning themselves on the boulders. Something about those rattlers bothered him. Not just that he'd almost been bitten by one. There was something else someone had told him.

Joining a line of wagons that clattered and squealed down the hillside, Mackenzie found the familiar footpath that led under the High Level Bridge and down to the Belly River.

The driftwood log looked lonely as Mackenzie walked across the empty beach to the shore. He glanced downstream but couldn't spot the family of ducks. The mother's hidden her babies, he decided.

"Hello," Mackenzie cried. "Captain! Ahoy! Are you there?"

Mackenzie remembered that when he was on the bridge, he saw the Captain building a ship. He listened for the crack of a hammer.

"Captain!" he called again.

Mackenzie turned at the sound of rustling in the bush behind him. Pushing through the last branches, the old man stepped onto the beach. He looked

Mackenzie up and down, smiled, and asked, "Are you a sailor?"

"No," Mackenzie said. "But I need to talk to you."

"It's not too late to sign on," the Captain said. "We'll be sailing soon."

"I can't," Mackenzie said. "I have to find my cousin. Francis. You know him."

Frowning, the man scratched the top of his head.

"He helped you buy things at Mister Finch's hardware," Mackenzie reminded him.

"For my ship!" the man said.

"Yes, sails and things," Mackenzie said. "Where is he?"

"Francis."

Is he playing stupid with me? Mackenzie wondered. "Where's Francis staying?" he asked, frustrated. "What's he doing? I have to see him."

"Only sailors live here by the river," the Captain said.

"But he was with you," Mackenzie said. "Why?"

"He's a good boy." Smiling, the old man drew his hand over his beard. "And clever. He helps me at the bank."

"I know that, too," Mackenzie said. "When he's not helping you, where is he?"

Looking toward the river, the man said, "The *Minnow* sails with the next high water."

"Why do you call it the *Minnow?*" Mackenzie asked.

"The *Minnow II*," the Captain said. "The first plied these waters thirty years ago." Touching his hand to his cap, he backed away from Mackenzie. "Avast, mate," he said. "I'm needed on board. We've lots to do to make her seaworthy." The next moment, he disappeared into the bush.

PUSHING AWAY A BROKEN BEAM, John Walter carefully lifted debris from Alfred's chest and legs. His friend looked tiny and fragile beside the immense heap of rock and timbers.

What am I supposed to do now? John Walter wondered. What do you do with a body?

Holding his lantern toward the entrance, John Walter tried to see through the wall of dust. Dipping his shoulders to protect his head, he made his way down the tunnel until he met a huge barricade.

More of the ceiling had collapsed here. Parts of the walls had caved in. Shards of the heavy braces lay scattered as if the wood had exploded. Boulders the size of barrels filled the entry. A thin stream of air flowed through a hole hidden somewhere in the mess and struck his face. Crawling from rock to rock, John Walter climbed the pile until, peering through the dim light of his lantern, he realized that the rubble completely filled the entry.

Plugged up solid, John Walter thought, as he stepped back onto the floor. I'm going to be here for awhile. From down the entry, he heard the sound of someone moaning. He found Alfred sitting up beside the remains of the barrow.

"You looked like you were dead," John Walter said, almost giggling with relief. "I found you buried under a pile of these rocks. When I pulled them off, I thought you were crushed."

"I feel like I was," Alfred said. "My chest hurts to breathe. My legs ache. What happened?"

"You don't remember?" John Walter asked, sitting down beside his friend. "There was a bump. A big one."

Alfred studied the mess in the light from John Walter's lantern.

"This is nothing," John Walter said. "The entry between here and the entrance is filled up. Totally, Alfred. Huge boulders."

"So, we can't get out?"

"Not by ourselves," John Walter said. "We'll have to wait."

"No one knows we're here."

"Sigurdson does," John Walter said. "He was going to check on us today or tomorrow. He knows his way all through this mine. He'll get us out."

"That old cheat?" Alfred said. "When he sees what's happened, he'll hightail it. We'll rot in here before he does anything."

"Francis, then," John Walter said. "Wherever he is."

"Did you tell your brother we were here?" Alfred asked.

"Not exactly," John Walter said. "What about your family? They'll notice you're gone."

"I told them I was staying with you for a few days,"

Alfred said. "John Walter, we have to find our own way out. Let's go look at the pile in the entry again."

"Let me light your lantern," John Walter said. "Mine's getting low."

"Too late," Alfred said. "I found it underneath me when I sat up. It's smashed to smithereens."

KICKING STONES FROM THE PATH, Mackenzie trudged homeward. I'm not looking for Francis anymore, he told himself. Wherever he is, he's hiding from me and everybody else. If he really wants to see me, he knows where I am. Mother wants to go back to Saskatoon soon after the baby's born. I probably won't talk to Francis again before we leave.

But I'll see John Walter. I should be nicer to him, Mackenzie thought. He *is* my cousin, too. I've probably spent more time with Ruth than with him. It wouldn't be so bad to do things together. Tomorrow we can go back to Galt Park. Or that other park he wanted to show me where some man keeps a pet bear. I'll ask him tonight.

MACKENZIE HEARD HIS MOTHER'S voice from outside the house. She didn't get angry very often. Or raise her voice at anyone.

"Ruth!" she cried, as Mackenzie came through the door. "What were you thinking? How could you put your mother through that?"

Ruth sat at the table, her downcast eyes stuck on her hands twisting together in her lap. "It's supposed to help bring the baby," she said.

"Who told you that?" Mackenzie's mother put her hands on her hips. "It sounds like some peasant medicine. Some old wives' tale."

"It was just something to try," Ruth said. "Nobody else –"

"I don't want to hear anymore of that," Mackenzie's mother interrupted. "You are not the only person in this house who is concerned about your mother. Every one of us wants to see her healthy and the baby safe."

"And I have to cook –"

"Ruth, please," Mackenzie's mother said.

Ruth didn't hear the rest of what her aunt said. She had already stormed past Mackenzie and out the door.

"Oh! Ruth!" Aunt Betsy's moan slid into the kitchen.

"She's gone, Betsy," Mackenzie's mother said, slumping into a chair. "I was too hard on her. I'm sorry. She'll be back."

Not knowing what to say, Mackenzie walked over to the counter and poured a glass of water. I'm not so sure, he thought.

Lethbridge Daily Herald

FRIDAY, AUGUST 23, 1912

BACHELOR MINERS RETURN WITH WIVES

Galicians Visited Old Country During Strike

Many of the Galicians who have toiled in the coal mines of this district have lived here for years while their wives and children remained in their home countries. These bachelor miners have lived in camp bunkhouses, sent most of their wages to their families, and waited for the day they could be united.

When the 1911 strike showed no sign of ending, the Galicians gathered up their savings from wherever they had them hidden, boarded a train heading east, and, once in Halifax, bought passage for Hamburg. A year later, they are making the trip back, this time with wives and babies in tow. As their husbands claim their own miners' houses for the first time, the Galician babas must quickly learn the language and customs of their new land.

CHAPTER SIX
Saturday, August 24, 1912

Curled up on a floor somewhere deep in the mine, John Walter woke to find sharp-edged stones digging into his sides. His mouth tasted of rock dust and bitter coal. It didn't help that there was water running somewhere close. The sound made him thirstier, more desperate for a drink of water. But Alfred was right. That water wasn't for drinking.

John Walter forced himself to open his eyes. The room was black, so dark the shapes near him cast no shadows. Reaching out a hand, he found Alfred and poked him.

"I'm awake." Alfred groaned. "I can't sleep. I ache all over."

"From when you were buried?" John Walter asked. "Shoot."

"I want to go back," Alfred said.

It's too late, John Walter thought. Somewhere

along the entry, his Wolf lamp lay abandoned, its light extinguished when the fuel ran out. Even if they still had its dim light, he knew he could never find his way back to the pile of rocks that blocked the entry. The boys had ventured down too many tunnels, in and out of too many rooms, around too many pillars, to ever remember the way.

John Walter felt the cool air slide over his forehead. Somehow, through all their twists and turns, the faint breeze had stayed with them. If there was a light, he could try again to find the source of the tiny wind. But how, in this blackness, could he know where to start?

Alfred moaned.

Hungry? John Walter asked silently. I am. If I knew where the food container was, I'd eat another potato in a second.

Let him get some sleep, John Walter told himself. He needs it. Running his tongue over his teeth, he tried to spit out the caked dust. I'd give anything, he thought, for a big glass of water.

THE BED HAD NOT BEEN SLEPT IN; Mackenzie was sure of that.

Downstairs, he heard his mother talking and his baby sister babbling in Aunt Betsy's room. The pot of porridge was half-full and creamy, the way his mother made it. Four bowls sat on the counter. Mackenzie pulled one toward him. All my cousins have gone, he thought. Every one of them.

The whole family must have known Uncle Jimmy was getting too sick to keep working, Mackenzie decided, and they each had an idea of what to do about it. Uncle Jimmy thought he'd get his oldest son to work in the mine. Francis would have none of it and took off. With her mother pregnant and then sick, Ruth was too busy taking care of her father and the house to do anything else. And John Walter? He always acted like he was older than his age. If his brother wouldn't be a miner, he would, Mackenzie realized.

Where? Mackenzie wondered. John Walter and Alfred would never get into the Number Three Mine, he knew. The only other place was one of the old abandoned collieries. But which one?

Mackenzie took a spoonful of porridge. It had cooled and congealed since he'd taken it from the pot. As he slowly ate the oatmeal, Mackenzie wondered how he was going to find his cousin's mine.

A MILE AWAY FROM THE HOUSE, John Walter raised his head and slowly turned it from side to side to ease the cramps in his neck. He needed water to wash the pellets of mud from his mouth. Spit wasn't enough. His stomach growled for food.

John Walter could just barely make out the darkened form of Alfred curled at his feet, the dynamite box pressed against his chest. John Walter wanted to give his friend a little nudge to make sure he was still alive, but he didn't know which end was head and which was feet.

"Alfred?" John Walter's voice croaked. He got lonely when his friend was so quiet. "You'll have to wake up sometime."

Carefully resting the back of his head against the rock wall, John Walter closed his eyes and waited again for sleep.

MACKENZIE PULLED THE DAY'S edition of the *Lethbridge Daily Herald* from the stack on the counter and started to read the news on page one. Mr. Smith had seen him enter the office. But, like Mackenzie's father, Mr. Smith was going to finish typing what he was writing before he spoke. Mackenzie flipped to an inside page.

Finally, Mr. Smith pushed away from his desk, slipped a pencil behind his ear, and joined Mackenzie at the counter.

"I thought I'd have seen your mother by now," Mr. Smith said. "No doubt she's busy with her sister. To what do I owe this pleasure?"

"Do you remember on Thursday there was an article about people stealing coal?" Mackenzie asked.

"Of course," Mr. Smith said. "That was one of my stories. Old Stevens was hopping mad about his losses."

"Do you know who was doing it?"

"I have my suspicions," Mr. Smith said. "No one's been nabbed in the act. Why do you ask?"

"Did I tell you before that my uncle is a miner?" Mackenzie asked.

Mr. Smith nodded.

"He has black lung and he can't work underground," Mackenzie said.

"Oh," Mr. Smith said. "That's a nasty business. I'm sorry to hear it, Mackenzie."

"My youngest cousin – he's only eight years old – and his friend decided to make some money for the family by digging coal."

Arching his eyebrows, Mr. Smith said, "Digging or stealing?"

"I don't know," Mackenzie said. "I don't want to get them in trouble. I just want to find them."

"They might be involved in taking coal from someone's mine," Mr. Smith said, rubbing his chin, "but two young boys could never carry that off on their own. You need tools and lamps and a wagon and someone who knows where to deliver the coal without getting caught. If they're digging in a mine, it's because some thieving adult has hired them to do it."

"Your article said it was dangerous working in an old mine," Mackenzie said.

"Yes, indeed," Mr. Smith said. "Too many men lost their lives in those early workings. That's why some of them were shut down. They just weren't safe. That's how some of them got their names, too. 'Widow's Mine,' things like that. Still, there are black-hearted men in this town who don't hesitate to send young lads into those places."

"Where are the mines?" Mackenzie asked.

"If you're thinking of going there," Mr. Smith said, "I'd like to come along but I'm up to my armpits in work. The editor would never let me out of his sight." As if to prove this, Mr. Smith pulled a watch out of his pocket and glanced at the face.

"They're not obvious," he said. "You have to look for them. Usually the entrance is hidden by trees or brush that's grown up since they were in use." He dropped the watch back into his pocket.

"The most likely workings for someone to get into," Mr. Smith said, "are dug into the side of the hill a half-mile or more north of the highway. If you go out towards the old cemetery, you'll find plenty of trails heading down into the valley."

Stepping away from the counter, Mr. Smith took a small bag from his pocket. "If you'll excuse me," he said. "I'd better get back to my story." Then, "Candy?"

Once again, the miners had been told there was no work for them in the mine. From his perch halfway up the railway embankment, Mackenzie could see the slumbering buildings of Galt Number Three and, in front of them, the old cemetery.

Would Mr. Smith tell him to walk across that prairie, Mackenzie wondered, if he knew it was infested with rattlesnakes? *Was* it infested with rattlesnakes? The only person to tell him that was John Walter.

But someone else had talked about rattlers. Aunt Betsy. Mackenzie remembered his aunt saying both boys in her family and their father were terrified of snakes. John Walter hadn't acted scared when he saw the rattler, even though the snake must have been as close to him as it was to Mackenzie. Staring at the prairie, Mackenzie tried to imagine that day on the trail. His eyes wandered to the edge of the valley and he imagined what Mr. Smith had said was down below.

There *was* no snake, he decided. John Walter had been trying to frighten him. He didn't want Mackenzie to venture into that part of the valley, for the same reason he'd told Mackenzie about the good things to do downtown instead. Now Mackenzie knew why: John Walter and Alfred were digging coal in the valley.

WHEN HE GOT TO THE PRAIRIE, Mackenzie spotted the rock John Walter had said sheltered the big rattler. Am I wrong? he wondered, feeling his chest tighten. Maybe there had been a snake. Maybe this meadow really was overrun with rattlers.

He raised his eyes to look further down the trail

and kept walking.

The pathway dropped down the steep side of the canyon and soon Mackenzie found himself studying the double ruts of wagon wheels that criss-crossed its flat, sandy bottom. Some of these might lead to John Walter's mine, Mackenzie thought.

But it was impossible to tell where one trail stopped and another started. Walking north, he kept the wall of the canyon in sight.

There it was! A path veered away toward the hillside. Getting closer, Mackenzie saw the ruts went behind a stand of trees. The mine's back there, he told himself. It's just like Mr. Smith said. Stopping to listen, he heard only the cries of a flock of small birds that dove recklessly through the branches of the trees.

The trail ended in a clearing, empty except for some crumbling balls of dry horse manure. Nearby, the charred remains of an old campfire lay scattered across a rocky ledge. There was no sign of a hole large enough to be a mine. Kicking a ball of manure into powdered dust, Mackenzie retraced his steps.

FIFTY YARDS FURTHER ALONG, following another track into another hidden clearing, Mackenzie discovered grey smoke curling from the embers of a recent fire and a dirty canvas tent with its front flap pegged open. Two jays hopped from the peak of the tent to peck the ground near a pair of boots that stuck out of the gap. A filthy, blackened wagon sat beside the fire and beyond that a grey nag was staked in a small meadow.

There was no sign of a mine entrance. Mackenzie backed away.

"JOHN WALTER!" ALFRED'S VOICE caught in his throat. Coughing, he tried to swallow some spit. "Look at this!"

Grimacing, John Walter slowly rubbed his neck and opened his eyes.

Alfred sat on the far side of the tunnel. He was a shadow, but John Walter could make out his arms and legs. And in the middle of Alfred's head, John Walter could see his friend's gleaming white teeth.

John Walter didn't care. It seemed like after hours of wakefulness, he had finally just fallen asleep. He didn't want to get up. He wanted to go back to sleep.

"What are you smiling at?" he asked.

"You, stupid," Alfred said. "How many fingers?"

"Holy cow!" John Walter said. "There's light in here. I can see you."

"It must be morning," Alfred said. "The light's coming down a hole somewhere." "I'm hungry," John Walter said. "Aren't you?"

Alfred patted the dynamite box. "I've got two more potatoes," he said. "But let's wait until we find the hole."

"I need water, too," John Walter said. "I've been

listening to a river running down a shaft all night. It can't be far."

"Get that idea out of your head," Alfred said. "You'll poison yourself drinking water from a mine. You have to wait for some good stuff. Cold and fresh. When we get out."

MACKENZIE FOUND HIS WAY to a clearing behind another grove of trees near the valley wall. Small bits of coal littered the short grass at the end of the wagon trail. Most of the nearby ground was rock and gravel, but there were footprints across a patch of sand. Mackenzie followed the tracks around a boulder.

A tunnel led into the hill, its mouth braced with many wooden timbers. A few steps closer, Mackenzie caught sight of John Walter's clothes. His cousin's black pants and red-checked shirt lay spread-eagled on a slab of rock. Nearby, another set of clothes waited for a boy the same size. Alfred, Mackenzie knew.

Mackenzie remembered John Walter scrubbing the coal dust on his hands and worrying about the dark smudges that stained his clothes. He hadn't wanted to get them dirty. The boys, Mackenzie decided, had found other clothes to wear while they dug coal.

They're inside the mine, Mackenzie decided. "John Walter!" he cried. "Alfred! You in there?" His voice, even its echo, was sucked into the cavern. There was no answer.

Mackenzie counted ten paces into the mine and then stopped to kneel down and pick up a piece of wood. By rapping his knuckles on the board and brushing away the flaking dirt, he could make out what was written on the sign: "Dead Man's Mine Stay Out!"

"John Walter?"

After twenty more steps, the dust in the darkened tunnel thickened enough to settle on his skin. It smelled sharp, like the air that bursts from a stone you smash into bits on a rock. Turning, Mackenzie peered through a hazy, grey screen that had fallen in front of the entrance. Already he was deeper into this mine than the one he'd entered with Francis. "John Walter!" Maybe they were working in a room, somewhere his voice wouldn't carry.

Mackenzie walked off more paces until he could no longer make out the walls of the entry or the ceiling or the floor. Bending down, he used his fingertips to dis-cover a jumble of rocks at his feet. Stretching out his arms, Mackenzie crawled over debris until he came to a wall of boulders. The pile seemed to fill the tunnel. He tugged on one of the rocks but it wouldn't move.

"John Walter!" Mackenzie cried. "Answer me!"

Mackenzie felt fear tighten his chest. The boys were trapped. He tried to imagine what it would be like on the other side of the rock fall.

How long have they been in there? Mackenzie wondered. Maybe a whole day. Do they have food? Water?

Mackenzie remembered what Uncle Jimmy had said about what it's like in a mine after a bump: blocked tunnels, coal dust, and deadly methane gas the men can't see or smell as it drifts toward them.

I need help, he told himself, stumbling toward the entrance. Once outside, Mackenzie sprinted for the trail that led to the prairie above.

Three blocks from the house, Mackenzie spotted Uncle Jimmy slouched in his chair. If the mine wasn't working today, his uncle probably hadn't started his new job. Slowing to a walk, Mackenzie thought about what he was going to say.

"HOW DO YOU KNOW THEY'RE in there?" Uncle Jimmy leaned forward, his hands on his knees, his elbows akimbo.

"It's their clothes," Mackenzie said, "I'm sure of it."

"Could be anywhere."

"I don't think so," Mackenzie said. "Every time I saw him the last few days he's been covered in coal dust. He must be working for someone, digging out coal that's going to be sold."

"Bloody stupid, that is," Uncle Jimmy said. "Why would he do that?"

"I think he was trying to help," Mackenzie said, and watched his uncle turn to him.

"John Walter knew you were going to lose your job as a contract miner," Mackenzie said. "Everybody did.

But I bet he didn't know you were going to get another job as a day man on the surface."

"Not a real job," Uncle Jimmy muttered, "for anyone who's been underground."

"When Francis left," Mackenzie said, "I think John Walter decided to be a coal miner himself. So he hooked up with someone who needed a couple of boys to dig out coal."

"When's the last time you saw John Walter?" Uncle Jimmy asked.

"Yesterday," Mackenzie said.

Uncle Jimmy sat upright. "Blasted kid," he said. "You didn't get any answer from inside?"

"No."

"Ruthie!" Uncle Jimmy bellowed. "Come here, love."

Carrying a glass, Ruth left the house and hurried toward the pump.

"Forget the water," Uncle Jimmy said. "Mack says John Walter has got himself trapped in one of the old mines. Him and Alfred."

Ruth looked at Mackenzie. He nodded.

"I need you to get over to Mr. Clarke's house. He'll be at home like the rest of us. Tell him what I just said and see if we can't meet in the empty lot beside his place. And get Mr. Shannon, too." Uncle Jimmy stood up, took a couple of shallow breaths, then deeper ones, holding his coughing in check.

"Mackenzie, I need you to get some things in the

house. We'll tell none of this to Betsy, mind you. Or your mother. They have enough to worry about. If I go in, Betsy will ask what's happening, and I don't want to have to lie to her. Then go park yourself in the field by Clarke's. The men will want to know what you told me. I'll meet you there. Then we'll see who knows his way around a coal mine."

MACKENZIE FOUND HIS MOTHER pacing in the hot, damp air inside the kitchen. She lifted the lid of a pot on the stove to see if the water was simmering. She walked to the table to count a stack of towels and then to the counter to shake out and refold baby blankets. She went into Aunt Betsy's room for a few seconds of murmured conversation. Returning, she headed to the stove.

"You're going to wear yourself out," Mackenzie said.

"Oh!" his mother said. "Where did you come from?"

"I can't stay," Mackenzie said, spying his uncle's water canteen.

"Have you seen Ruth?" Mackenzie's mother asked, frowning at the towels. "She's disappeared. We may need her soon."

"She's probably not far," Mackenzie said. "I'm going with Uncle Jimmy for awhile."

"That's a blessing," his mother said. "Poor Jimmy just isn't himself. It'll do him good to get away from the house."

Mackenzie waited until his mother had completed her routine and started for the bedroom. He rummaged behind the door and tucked a blanket under his arm before leaving the house.

THE FIRST PERSON TO SHOW UP at the empty lot was a short man with a miner's broad shoulders and a face that looked familiar to Mackenzie.

"I've just come from Jimmy's house," the man said. "The missus wanted me to give her regards. They don't know, do they?"

"No."

"Just as well," the man said. "Be a terrible shock in her state. Jimmy said the boys got themselves into one of the old mines. I'm surprised. I thought they were locked up pretty tight. Alfred and me have been all through the bottoms there, looking for old arrowheads. He never showed any interest in going inside when he was with me."

That's why you look familiar, Mackenzie thought. "Are you Alfred's father?" he asked.

"Yes. Sorry, lad," the man said. "I didn't introduce myself." He put out his hand to shake. "I know who you are, of course. In a place like this, it's easy to spot the one who's not from a mine family. I should thank you, too. Jimmy told me you're the one who sorted this out."

"You're welcome. How will you find them?"

"We won't know until we're inside and see what's

happened." Alfred's father sat on the stoop and, by nodding his head, told Mackenzie to as well.

How can he be so calm, Mackenzie wondered. He and Uncle Jimmy both. I thought we'd run right back and start digging, with our hands if we had to.

As if he knew what Mackenzie was thinking, Alfred's father said, "Waiting's always hard, Mack, whether you're inside or out. First thing you learn is to be patient. Wait and do it right. Doesn't help anyone to rush around like a chicken with its head cut off. Jimmy's got Shannon and Clarke at it. Two of the best mine rescue men in all of the Crowsnest."

More men began arriving, each one finding his way to Alfred's father, where they talked quietly and shook one another's hands. Then the men split into clusters of three or four to talk among themselves. Mackenzie heard foreign words and accented English spoken in many of the groups. Thirsty from his run, he took a sip from the canteen.

"Who would do such a thing?" one man asked. "Send two boys into an old mine on their own."

"No miner," another man answered. "You can bet on that."

"We can only hope the boys had enough sense to stay put," a man pointed out. "If they've been wandering in there for twenty-four hours, it could take days to find them."

"That might not be soon enough," another added, "if the damp's found its way in."

"Here's Shannon," a man interrupted. "Give him room."

The miners quickly gathered around the new man. Mackenzie joined them at the edge of the circle. Going up on tiptoes, it took him a few moments to follow the sound of dry coughing and find Uncle Jimmy, looking grim near the centre of the group. In a low voice, Mr. Shannon told the miners what their jobs would be. He's like a baseball coach, Mackenzie thought, telling each player the position he'll play.

It was the middle of the morning when most of the men started walking toward the valley. They carried tools over their shoulders, or hauled lanterns or water containers or blankets and old sheets that Mackenzie figured out were going to be used for patching up injuries. Another group hopped on a wagon, and the driver urged his team onto the road that led to the Number Three Mine.

Already forgotten by the miners, Mackenzie found a place for himself at the end of a group of rescuers.

ONCE THE MEN HAD SEEN THE ROCK FALL, Mr. Clarke and Mr. Shannon divided the miners into groups who would take turns digging at the pile. The wagon that had gone to the Number Three Mine appeared and was swarmed immediately by a gang of men who lifted off heavy timbers as easily as broom handles. No sooner was the bracing stacked near the entrance than

Mr. Clarke had men haul the lumber into the mine to begin to shore up the broken ceiling.

As news spread through the mining neighbourhoods, more miners and their families showed up. Miners' wives gathered branches from the valley floor and lit fires under the sheltering trees. The women balanced cooking pots over the flames and shooed away their young children to play in the valley nearby. Older children were dispatched to the river.

Every few minutes Uncle Jimmy walked into the mine entrance, but each time he was driven back by rasping coughs that doubled him over as he retreated outside. Alfred's father found the waiting easier when he moved from fire to fire and group to group, thanking the miners for their help.

The teams didn't spend long in the mine before being replaced. Those coming out told of clearing the smaller debris with their bare hands and smashing the larger chunks into pieces that could be moved. The progress was steady, they said. Each team reported how much closer they were to breaking through.

Mackenzie felt out of place. What did Alfred's father mean when he said he could tell Mackenzie wasn't from a mine family? The people in the clearing looked at him almost suspiciously out of the corners of their eyes, he thought. It's like they think this is my fault. Turning his back on the miners, Mackenzie walked along the wall of the valley and then climbed up the hillside. There was no path to follow. He had to grab onto the stalk of a low bush or grip his boot against a rock to go higher. About twenty yards up, he shuffled back across the side of the canyon until he came to a dip in the hill that made a natural chair. From here he could see the mine entrance below him and both ways down to the valley floor. Glancing up, Mackenzie saw the sun had already passed its high point in the sky and was sliding down toward the western horizon. Soon it'll be heating up this hillside, he thought, settling into the little gulley.

OLE SIGURDSON AWOKE FULLY DRESSED in his little tent, which now felt like the inside of an oven. Sitting up, he rubbed a finger under his red bandana. Sigurdson reached for his hat and crawled out of the tent.

The sound of voices had wakened him. It was odd, he knew, for people to gather in this part of the valley. Getting his bearings, he decided the people talking were nearby. He walked to the grove of trees that hid his camp and peered between the branches. Streams of people were walking to and from the mine he'd been taking coal out of. Snugging his hat on his forehead, Sigurdson stepped out from behind the trees and followed two women toward the mine.

As he got closer, he counted at least fifty people in the nearby valley. About half of them, he guessed from their clothes, were miners. Two other men stood out by their red serge jackets and stiff brown hats. The

Mounties were facing away from him, talking to a small group of men. Kneeling, Sigurdson pretended to tie the laces of his boots and soon heard what he wanted of the bystanders' conversations.

Two boys were trapped inside the mine. No one knew how long they'd been in there. Mine rescue teams were working non-stop. The miners expected to find the boy's bodies when they cleared a huge rock fall from the mine entry.

Sigurdson stood up. Whatever those two young brats had done to make the tunnel collapse, he was sure to be blamed for it. Letting his gaze wander, the merchant noticed a boy sitting by himself on the hillside. The boy's attention was drawn to some sort of commotion at the mine entrance. A good time to leave, Sigurdson thought. Turning his head away whenever he met someone, he returned to his camp.

JOHN WALTER AND ALFRED PEERED up the tunnel that started on the floor of the shaft and rose above their heads, on and on up to a tiny pinprick of light.

"Where does it go, do you think?" Alfred asked. "Where does it come out?"

"I'm so turned around, I can't tell," John Walter said. "Maybe up on the prairie."

"Tunnel's awful narrow," Alfred said. "You wouldn't want to get stuck."

"Those old miners must have dug out this air hole,"

John Walter said. "If it was big enough for them, it'll be big enough for us."

"Are you going first?" Alfred asked.

"Let's have those potatoes," John Walter said, "and then I'll be ready."

THE NEWS SPREAD LIKE A BLAST shooting down the tunnel and out the entrance. Hearing the words was enough to take away each bystander's breath. The miners had broken through! Without prompting, everyone in the valley moved toward the entrance. Were the boys alive? That was the question on everyone's lips.

The answer: maybe. The boys hadn't been buried by the collapse. There were no more rock falls in the entry and nearby rooms. No dangerous levels of dust or methane gas were found. But this part of the old mine was empty. The boys had gone further inside.

Mr. Clarke and Mr. Shannon brought all the miners out to sit together with Uncle Jimmy and Alfred's father. Mackenzie climbed down the hill until he could easily hear what was said.

Alfred's father held up a battered, almost flattened piece of metal. "One of the men found my old can-teen," he said. "It leaks a bit so I stopped using it but Alfred likes to take it with him. The lads are inside. I'm sure of it."

"Who's to tell where they've ended up?" Mr.

Shannon said. "There could be a dozen old rooms in there. Each one has to be searched."

"The bump's bound to have done damage further in," a miner said. "The old timbers can't hold up. They're as brittle as kindling. You're going to find more rock falls."

"That won't be the end, either," a man said. "This whole hillside is unstable. Right over to Number Three. That won't be the last bump we'll see."

"If another one comes," a voice said, "it won't be just two boys caught inside."

Mackenzie studied the faces of the miners. Many looked tired, disheartened, their eyes cast down to the ground. What will they do? he wondered. Is it too dangerous to go further inside looking for John Walter and Alfred?

"So," one of the miners said in a soft voice, "we know what we're up against, then." He looked around the circle. "This is nothing any of us hasn't done before. Or had done for us. Jimmy here was the first man I saw coming to get me after the bump at Bellevue. If he hadn't led us out when he did, they'd have carried me out for sure. I'm going back in. And I swear I won't leave this forsaken hole until we find those boys."

"I'll be there," another man said.

"Can't stop us," a miner added.

A chorus of similar voices, many in heavily accented English, echoed over the clearing.

"We'll start in one hour," Mr. Clarke said. "We need to refill the lanterns. The ladies are determined to feed us. Get some rest if you can; we may be here for a long while yet."

"WHAT'S IT LIKE?" ALFRED called. "How far up are you?"

"It's a snap," John Walter hollered back. "Like climbing a ladder. I'm halfway at least."

"Can you see anything yet?"

"No," John Walter said. "But it's getting brighter. The sun's coming in. Don't just sit there, Alfred. Start climbing."

"I will," Alfred said. "But you're knocking down tons of dirt. I don't want to eat it all the way up."

"Well, hurry," John Walter said. "I'm almost there. But..."

Alfred waited. "But what?" he said.

"But," said John Walter, sounding discouraged, "something's blocking the way out."

THE MINER'S WIFE DIDN'T GIVE Mackenzie a second glance. He was one of dozens of people lined up for a bowl of stew and a slice of freshly baked bannock. After wolfing down the meal, Mackenzie's stomach ached for more. Thinking of Alfred and John Walter, he returned the bowl and climbed back to his lookout.

The gulley wasn't as cozy as he remembered. There were pebbles digging into his seat and back. No matter how he shifted his weight, the little stones still poked him. Clambering to his hands and knees, Mackenzie brushed the pebbles out of the depression and got himself comfortable again.

The first teams of rescuers were back in the mine. Working in pairs, the men were going to follow the entry, search any rooms they came to, and bring back the information so Mr. Shannon could add it to the map he was creating.

More people arrived at the site, including a handful of men in black suits. From his perch, Mackenzie watched the businessmen move sombrely around the clearing murmuring sympathy to the miners. After a few minutes, the newcomers walked away in the direction of the valley road. From behind a clump of trees, Mackenzie heard a sputtering motorcar being cranked to life. Soon the putt-putt sound of the vehicle's engine faded into the distance.

There's Mr. Smith! Mackenzie recognized the reporter and his long moustache as he strode into the clearing with his notebook open and his pencil at the ready. Mackenzie caught his eye and waved but Mr. Smith had found Mr. Clarke and, as Mackenzie watched, he took the elbow of the rescue leader and guided him to a quieter spot.

A small stone rolled down the hillside, bounced off a ledge, and cracked into a rock beside Mackenzie.

Reaching over to pick up the missile, he barely had time to take a look at it before another stone struck the rock.

Mackenzie twisted around. The hillside above him looked like every other part of the canyon wall: scattered boulders half-buried in the dirt, spindly bushes clinging to the rocky ground, and bunches of yellow grass that must have died when the rains had stopped months ago in the spring.

Another stone was heading his way! This one struck a patch of loose gravel on the way down, sparking a small, dusty landslide that rattled past Mackenzie. There's something strange going on, Mackenzie thought. Pushing himself up, he studied the place the slide had started. He began to climb.

RUTH SAT ON THE STOOP WITH her ear pressed against the screen door. Nothing was happening, she decided.

They were out of time. The birth had to start or her mother might die.

Ruth jumped to her feet. Nadia would know what to do next.

MACKENZIE WALKED ACROSS THE PLATEAU he had found further up the valley wall, a level place about the size of his bed. He must have been mistaken. There was nothing here that would cause rocks to suddenly cascade down the hill. Far away, the High Level Bridge soared over the canyon. Down on the bottom, he could see the sandy island he had explored with John Walter. At the base of the hill, the miners and their wives stood waiting near the mine entrance.

As he turned away from the level place, Mackenzie caught sight of a headland jutting out from the hillside near the top of the valley. If I stand on that monster, he thought, I'll be able to see further. He continued his climb.

THERE WAS SPACE FOR TWO small bodies under the boulder sitting on top of the air hole. Through an opening under the huge rock, John Walter could see blue sky and the sun that would soon fall below the far side of the canyon. If he mashed his face into the boulder, he could make out the upper branches of the tallest trees in the valley. Out a hole on the other side, Alfred saw only a few feet of hill.

"Let me look for awhile," Alfred said. "You've had enough time."

"There's nothing," John Walter said. "I don't know where these stones are ending up, but there can't be anybody below us. We need to go back down this hole and see if there's another way out. This was a waste of time."

"Just move," Alfred said. "I want a turn. Then we can go down."

Being careful to find footholds in the rocks, John Walter climbed away from the opening. "You could try shouting," he said.

"Who would hear?" Alfred asked, moving into John Walter's old position. After glancing out the opening, Alfred pushed his face under the edge of the boulder to suck in hot, fresh air.

"Seen enough, yet?" John Walter asked.

"I don't recognize anything," Alfred said. "It all looks the same from up here."

"We should get going while there's still some daylight," John Walter said.

"One more minute," Alfred said. "I just got here."

RUTH BURST INTO THE KITCHEN, her hands clenched in tight fists at her sides and a fierce look in her eyes. Behind her, a stranger glided around the room from counter to stove to table. Carrying a bag on her arm, the woman nodded at Ruth and then turned to a startled Aunt Maude and smiled.

"This is Nadia," Ruth said. "She's going to help Mother."

Mackenzie's mother stared at her niece.

"Mother needs to start having her baby," Ruth went on. "Nadia is going to break her water."

"But," Aunt Maude said, "we need a doctor for that."

"There's no time anymore," Ruth said. Out of the corner of her eye, she saw Nadia drift across the kitchen and enter her mother's room. "She's going to examine Mother," she said.

"Who is she?" Mackenzie's mother whispered. "Where did she come from?"

"She's the neighbour," Ruth said, "from the pretty house."

"The one your mother doesn't like?"

"She doesn't know that, Aunt Maude. Mother's never talked to her."

"This may not be the best time to start," Mackenzie's mother said.

Nadia came back into the kitchen and took a folded cloth from her bag. Opening the cloth on her palm, she exposed a thin, shiny steel instrument which Ruth glimpsed as it slid into the pot of boiling water.

"Momma is ready," Nadia said. Looking up, she smiled again at Mackenzie's mother before using what looked like a dinner fork to lift the steel instrument from the water and place it on the cloth. She walked into the bedroom with Ruth and Aunt Maude in tow.

Keeping her instrument out-of-sight, Nadia murmured softly to Aunt Betsy. She crossed the room and started to close the door. "I am busy now," Nadia said. "Auntie too. Sometimes it is noisy. Sometimes quiet. The door is closed until Auntie comes to get you. Boil more water, Ruth. When we are finished, we have some tea."

Ruth returned to the kitchen, sat at the table, and rested her head on her arms to wait.

"I'M STARTING DOWN," John Walter said.

"I'm coming, too."

"We'll find something else," John Walter said, trying to sound hopeful.

"We should've just stayed at the entry." Alfred flung a handful of pebbles through a gap below the boulder.

A dark cloud passed over the opening. The boys heard the sound of breathing. Someone crouched beside the boulder, blocking the sun. A shadowed face filled the opening.

"John Walter?" a voice asked in disbelief. "Alfred? Is that you in there?"

IT WAS MINERS WHO HAD ROLLED the boulder years ago to block the air hole and keep people out of the abandoned mine. It was miners who, with bare hands, picks, and shovels, chipped their way back into the hole to pull out John Walter and Alfred. Each boy was quickly snatched into the firm embrace of his own father before being passed around the relieved crowd to receive a hug, a hand shake, or a friendly cuff on the back of the head.

Mackenzie held back. A few of the miners patted his shoulder, but it was John Walter and Alfred, sons of miners, they wanted to hear from.

A procession of miners and miners' wives led the boys to the base of the hill. There, each one hungrily drank a quart of cold water and devoured as much stew as was dolloped into his bowl. John Walter and Alfred were then sat down by one of the fires. In the weakening light they were peppered with the questions that had been hanging over the old mine. Soon heads began to nod – "Just as I thought," they said – as the adults heard the story of the conniving Ole Sigurdson and his boy miners.

Standing at the back of the crowd, Mackenzie listened too, until he was nudged by a newcomer. Thinking the man wanted to get closer, Mackenzie stepped aside. The man then grabbed Mackenzie's sleeve and dragged him out of the firelight.

"Francis!" Mackenzie grinned at his cousin. "Where have you been?"

"It's a long story," Francis said. "What's going on? I've been hearing people coming and going all day but I was too busy to find out what was happening. What have those two been up to?"

"You don't know?" Mackenzie asked. "John Walter and Alfred have been trapped in this old mine for over a day. We just got them out."

"What were they doing in there?" Francis asked.

"They've been working for Ole Sigurdson."

"Sigurdson!" Francis was quiet for a moment. "Were they trying to make some money?"

Mackenzie nodded.

"That's my fault!" Francis said. "After I left home, Mackenzie, Sigurdson saw me downtown and asked me to work for him. I knew all about his ways and I refused. When he kept pestering me, I told him no matter how poor we got, I'd never work for him. I wouldn't let my little brother work for him. I never should have mentioned my brother. I was just trying to be smart. I bet that's when he went after the boys. John Walter would be no match for Sigurdson's lies and promises."

"They're all right now," Mackenzie said.

"What a blackguard!" Francis said.

"You're not the only one angry with Sigurdson," Mackenzie said. "Some of these people sound like they're ready to lynch him."

"He'll weasel out of it somehow," Francis said. "Look, Mackenzie, I'm sorry I can't stay. I have to go right away."

"Where? Why can't you tell me?"

"I'll write you. I'll let you know. Soon." Francis squeezed Mackenzie's shoulder and quickly turned away. Mackenzie watched him disappear into the dusk.

Back at the campfire, John Walter saw through blurry eyes that Alfred had collapsed against his father. Teetering beside his own father, John Walter's head grew heavier, tipped toward his chest and then jerked upright again.

"Come lads," Uncle Jimmy said, noisily stifling a cough. "It's time to get home. You can have a good long sleep when you're back in your own beds."

A CLOUD OF STEAM HISSED BENEATH the coach as the conductor put one foot on his stool, looked down the empty, dimly lit platform and called, "All aboard!"

A lone passenger hurried from the station, his ticket clasped in one hand, a small valise in the other.

"Evening," the conductor said, stepping back on the platform long enough for the man to climb the steps. Reaching down, the conductor scooped up his stool.

The coach was only half full. But, hoping to stretch out in sleep, the passengers who had arrived twenty minutes earlier had spread themselves over every available space. Finally, at the far end of the coach, the newcomer found a vacant seat. As he sat down, he felt the train jerk ahead and then slowly begin its long trip into the night.

Stifling a yawn with his hand, the conductor made his way down the aisle. He took the new passenger's ticket without speaking, clicked it with his hole puncher, and after quickly counting the passengers, headed to the door that led to the next coach.

Sliding his finger beneath his bandana, Ole Sigurdson sighed. He was bitter about leaving Lethbridge, and angry he'd had to sell his wagon and old nag so quickly. The ticket in the merchant's pocket read "Vancouver". But long before the train reached the ocean, probably in some coalmining town in the mountains to the west, he planned to take his own exit from the coach.

FRANCIS STOOD OUTSIDE the back door, his eyes closed, his hand on the knob. A single lantern, turned low, cast a faint light over the kitchen and through the screen. The only noise he could hear from inside the house was the sound of someone softly snoring. Francis slipped through the door and tiptoed into the kitchen.

Ruth slept at the table. Across from her, Aunt Maude slouched against the back of her chair, her mouth open, her breathing deep. Francis noticed the pot of water steaming on the stove and the pile of towels on the counter. He walked into the bedroom.

His mother was asleep, too, her head and shoulders propped on pillows, her hair damp and stringy. Francis reached across to the dresser, picked up a towel, and softly wiped his mother's wet forehead.

As her eyes fluttered open, Francis's mother smiled. "Thank you," she whispered.

"You're awake," Francis said.

"What's happening?" his mother asked. "Have you come home? Are you going to stay?"

Francis shook his head. "I came to say goodbye," he said. "I'm off to seek my fortune."

"You don't need to do that," Francis's mother said. "Your father feels differently about things. His anger's gone."

"I'm decided," Francis said. "How are you feeling, Mother?"

"I look terrible, I know," his mother said. "I can see

it in your face. Don't worry. Two days of sleep and I'll be on my feet again."

"I knew you'd come back to see her." Ruth stood in the doorway, a teacup in her hand.

"Hello, sister."

"If you're awake, you're supposed to drink this, Mother," Ruth said. "And then have a feeding."

"This is what it's like now, Francis," his mother said, a smile playing on her lips. "I swear Ruth memorizes everything the midwife says."

"I'll get out of your way," Francis said, walking toward the door.

"Did you even look at her?" Ruth's voice sounded cross. Handing the cup to her mother, she knelt by a wooden butter box draped with a towel. Lifting a bundle to her shoulder, she returned to Francis and unfolded the blanket. "A healthy girl," she said.

Francis studied the tiny creature, his face softening. "She looks like you," he said.

"My face isn't wrinkly like that!"

"You know what I mean," Francis said. Stroking the baby's cheek, he turned his ear to the door. The sound of voices carried into the house from the street.

"Goodbye." Bending down to kiss his mother's forehead, Francis hurried out of the house.

Lethbridge Daily Herald

SATURDAY, AUGUST 24, 1912

RATTLERS EYEING LETHBRIDGE REAL ESTATE

Local Vipers Like Coulee Bottoms and Short-grass Prairie

The number of sightings of Prairie Rattlesnakes near our city is on the rise this summer, due perhaps to the continuing hot weather and the abundance of gophers and mice. According to one wrangler who has ridden herd all across the southern prairies, rattlers are timid and prefer to remain unseen. Only when they are surprised or cornered will rattlers try to strike.

"It's a frightening thing to see a big rattler when he's threatened," the cowpoke told this reporter. "He can strike in all directions and throw himself about half his own body length. Some old rattlers can grow to almost five feet long and weigh over four pounds, so you don't want to be close when he decides to protect himself."

Prairie Rattlesnakes have their favourite dens to spend the winters and they don't stray too far in the summer. They like river and coulee bottoms, badlands, sage flats, and short-grass prairies.

CHAPTER SEVEN
Monday, August 26, 1912

Mackenzie stepped outside, leapt over his mother's trunk sitting near the stoop, and strode to Uncle Jimmy's chair. Halting there, Mackenzie looked down the street that would take them to the Overhead Bridge and the railway station. There wasn't a buggy in sight. Pivoting round, he marched back to the door. He knew he was being foolish, but now that they were going home, he wanted to get started.

As he entered the kitchen, he met his mother walking the baby, gently rocking the swaddled bundle and cooing into her tiny ear. Catching Mackenzie's eye, his mother nodded toward her feet. Nellie clung to her dress, looking unhappy and confused. Bending down, Mackenzie scooped up his sister and ran his fingers down her ribs until she giggled and took her eyes off her mother.

"Where's John Walter?" Mackenzie asked. He was sure his cousin had been in the kitchen a minute ago.

"Off to Alfred's, I suppose," Aunt Betsy said from her room. "He is grateful, Mackenzie. It's just hard for him to keep still."

"I know," Mackenzie said, rolling Nellie off his chest to hold her upside down by her ankles.

MACKENZIE AND JOHN WALTER and Uncle Jimmy had spent a couple of hours together on Sunday afternoon, once they were all up from their long sleeps.

"I should have cottoned on to what you rascals were up to and put a stop to it," Uncle Jimmy had said to John Walter. "Mind, I'd have thought you'd have enough sense not to venture into such a place."

"Alfred and I could have made a lot of money," John Walter said.

"No matter how much coal you dug," Uncle Jimmy said, "Sigurdson would have found a way to rob you of your pay. No. You're halfway to sixteen already, John Walter. You don't have long to wait until you can be a real miner. Maybe in Number Three or one of the new collieries they're building in the Crowsnest. That would be a grand job."

Patting Mackenzie on the knee, Uncle Jimmy said, "And it's your cousin, who doesn't even like the inside of a mine, we have to thank for getting you lads rescued." He looked at John Walter and nodded.

"Thanks," John Walter said.

"You're welcome," Mackenzie said. "What are you and Alfred going to do now?"

"Catch more gophers," John Walter said. "There's lots of them out by the old cemetery."

Later, when they'd been lying in bed waiting to go to sleep, John Walter had changed his mind. "We knew what we were doing, Alfred and me," he said. "Another couple of minutes and we would've got ourselves out of that air hole. We didn't need your help."

Mackenzie had kept quiet. He knew how much John Walter wanted to be grown up. He rolled onto his knees to look out the window. A rabbit was visiting his aunt's garden, nibbling, hopping along a row and then stopping to eat again. "Goodbye," Mackenzie whispered. The lonely wail of a locomotive whistle carried across the prairie. Stretching out on his back on the cot, Mackenzie had clasped his hands behind his head and thought about the train ride home.

NELLIE SQUEALED IN MACKENZIE'S HANDS. He hoisted her onto his shoulder.

Hours earlier, he'd heard Uncle Jimmy leave the house and join other men speaking quietly to each other on their way to start their morning shifts. He hadn't come back. He must be a day man now, Mackenzie decided. He was ready to be a bone picker.

The screen door slapped shut, and a moment later

Ruth walked in carrying a willow basket. Lifting a brightly embroidered white cloth, she held the basket up to Mackenzie.

Mackenzie sniffed the baking inside, smiled, and plucked out two of the delicious balls. "I remember these," he said, handing one to Nellie. "Poppy seeds. Almonds. Mmm."

"It's *pampushky*," Ruth said.

"What are you talking about?" Aunt Betsy asked. Mackenzie smiled. It seemed strange to have her chatting as if she was in the same room. But it was nice to have his aunt part of the family again.

"They're like doughnuts," Ruth said. "Very sweet. Nadia made them for us." Handing one to Mackenzie's mother, Ruth disappeared into the bedroom. "She said to tell you she's coming over in a few minutes to check on you." A moment later, Ruth was back.

"How did you get to be friends with that woman?" Mackenzie's mother asked.

"After Mother got really big with the baby," Ruth said, "whenever I went outside, I'd see Nadia watching through the window. One day she asked me in to try some baking." Ruth dropped a whole *pampushky* into her mouth. "She was a midwife in the old country so she started giving me things for Mother."

"You never told me any of that," Aunt Betsy said.

The talk was making Mackenzie feel uncomfortable. He went outside.

"I knew what you'd say, Mother," Ruth said. "When

you started getting puffy, Nadia knew it was your blood pressure. She gave me the raspberry tea and the castor oil to try to make the baby come faster."

"And when that didn't work," Mackenzie's mother said, "she broke your water. And probably saved your life."

"Have you picked a name yet?" Ruth asked.

"I know what you're getting at," Aunt Betsy said. "I'll talk to your father."

Mackenzie stuck his head in the door. "There's a buggy coming up the street," he said. "It's probably our cab. I'll help him with the trunk."

A few minutes later, with the taxi waiting, Mackenzie's mother hugged Ruth and handed over the baby. "I won't doubt you again," she told her niece. "I know you'll take good care of things."

"Not by myself, I hope," Ruth said. "Mother says she'll make John Walter help me." She shrugged. "Maybe he will."

"Get in here, Mackenzie!" Aunt Betsy called. "You're not escaping that easily."

Mackenzie found his aunt sitting up in bed, her arms thrown out to her sides. "Come," she said, wrapping her arms around Mackenzie and pressing her lips onto his forehead until he felt her tears wet his cheek.

"We'll be back," Mackenzie said, pulling away from his aunt.

"I know you will," she said. "And I won't let you near any coal mine!"

September 2, 1912

Dear Mackenzie,

Yesterday we arrived in Medicine Hat on the Captain's ship (really just a raft!). When we first left Lethbridge, we had to pole her through shallow water. That was hard work. Then the floodwaters caught up to us, the Captain set the sail to catch the wind, and we sat and enjoyed the ride.

We pulled up on shore near where the first Minnow docked years ago. The Captain is happy to be back. He thinks he might stay here for awhile.

This morning I met a man who stopped me on the sidewalk and offered me a job. Mr. Douglas owns a big farm and he is looking for men to help him run it. He moved here from Ohio last year and already he has built the largest house in these parts. He is a modern farmer. When I go to live on his homestead he will teach me how to operate all the newest machinery he owns.

Yes, Mackenzie, I will be a farmer. Soon I will start to make my fortune!

Give my regards to your family. I'll write again after the harvest.

Your cousin,
Francis

Acknowledgements

People offered advice and assistance to me at many stages of the writing of this novel. The story is the better for it.

The staff of the University of Saskatchewan Archives and the Galt Museum and Archives in Lethbridge provided many documents that helped me understand the historical context of *Danger in Dead Man's Mine.*

The staff of the Bellevue Underground Mine Tours in Bellevue, Alberta, spent a lot of time filling me in on the workings of a mine, especially the collieries operating in the Crowsnest Pass in the early years of the twentieth century. I have a special thanks for Kate Hanson for setting up my visit to Bellevue. If you, too, are interested in learning about old mines, the Bellevue Underground Mine Tours are a great place to start.

Larry Warwaruk alerted me to a potential problem in the plot. Lennie Mac Isaac, Judy Mac Isaac and Diane Peterson kindly read the manuscript with a critical eye on my interpretation of the lives of miners and the state of the mines. Lennie also generously shared stories of his own mining experiences, one of which made it into the manuscript. Dr. Sarah Glaze clarified for me Aunt Betsy's perilous condition.

Geoffrey Ursell applied his usual precise editing skills to the final versions of the manuscript.

About the Author

DAVE GLAZE IS THE AUTHOR of five previous Coteau juvenile novels, including *The Last Flight of the Birdman*, *The Light-Fingered Gang*, *Pelly* and *Waiting for Pelly*. *The Last Flight of the Birdman* and *Waiting for Pelly* have both been nominated for a Diamond Willow Award in the Saskatchewan Young Readers' Choice Book Awards. *Pelly* has been adopted for use in many schools across the country, including the entire Newfoundland education system. Dave Glaze has spent most of his life in Saskatoon. Recently retired, he worked for twenty-five years as a teacher, librarian and an educational consultant.

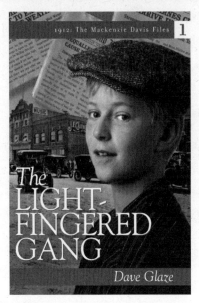

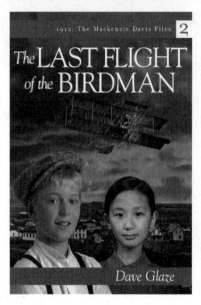

The production of ***Danger in Dead Man's Mine*** on Rolland Enviro 100 Print paper instead of virgin fibres paper reduces Coteau Book's ecological footprint by :

Tree(s) : 9
Solid waste : 252 kg
Water : 23 825 L
Suspended particles in the water : 1,6 kg
Air emissions : 553 kg
Natural gas : 36 m³

100%

PERMANENT

Printed on Rolland Enviro 100, containing 100% post-consumer recycled fibers, Eco-Logo certified, Processed without chlorinate, FSC Recycled and manufactured using biogas energy.